To Cristin
We live to

Over Come.

With Love

TRAVESTY

Margie Shepherd

Order this book online at www.trafford.com
or email orders@trafford.com

Most Trafford titles are also available at major online book retailers.

© Copyright 2007, 2008, 2010 Margie Shepherd.
All rights reserved. No part of this publication may be reproduced, stored in a retrieval
system, or transmitted, in any form or by any means, electronic, mechanical, photocopying,
recording, or otherwise, without the written prior permission of the author.

Printed in the United States of America.

ISBN: 978-1-4251-8731-6 (sc)
ISBN: 978-1-4269-8030-5 (e)

*Our mission is to efficiently provide the world's finest, most comprehensive book publishing
service, enabling every author to experience success. To find out how to publish your book,
your way, and have it available worldwide, visit us online at www.trafford.com*

Trafford rev. 10/18/2010

 www.trafford.com

North America & international
toll-free: 1 888 232 4444 (USA & Canada)
phone: 250 383 6864 ♦ fax: 812 355 4082

DELCOTATION

"MY NAME IS MARGIE SHEPHERD.
I AM THE PLAINTIFF.
I AM THE AUTHOR AND VICTIM.
THE FOLLOWING IS MY OPINION!"

Editor's Note: Inspired by a true story, this book is a work of non fiction!

DEDICATION

With love to my grandchildren, Nate, Ana, and Alexander,
and to all people through out the world who have
experienced **travesty**.

"I am both holding on and letting go!"

—*Margie Shepherd, 2010*

"It's not how hard you can hit, but how hard of a hit you can take and keep on going."

—*Margie Shepherd, 2010*

"Describe in one word your DNA for success—**tenacity**."

—*Margie Shepherd, 2010*

"Please outline the definition of your DNA for success in five words—**belief, faith, possibilities, commitment and integrity**."

—*Margie Shepherd, 2010*

FOREWORD

Approximately 30 years ago I met Margaret "Margie" Shepherd, an energetic, beautiful woman, and we immediately formed a strong friendship that has lasted ever since. From the 1970s into the early part of this century, Margie always had a smile, ready to laugh and enjoy life to its fullest. The travesty that Margie has gone through these past three years has changed her life immensely, a different woman than the lady I met those many years ago.

Even though Margie and I did not see each other much for a couple of years we kept track of each other through a mutual friend. Early in this decade, Margie and I reunited in Reno, Nevada, after each of us coincidentally moved to that region. As before, upon our initial reunion, she remained a vivacious, fun, laughing woman.

Yet since the travesty that hit Margie's life in 2005, she has touched my heart to such a degree that the change has been difficult to describe. My friend has struggled to get back to the same person she had been those years back. As Margie tells me all of the time, the word "no" is not in her vocabulary, and it isn't. Whenever Margie hears that word, she just keeps fighting. Filled with admiration, I would like to have half her drive.

I hope you will see through reading this book what a great person she is, and maybe learning her story will inspire you to think of someone you know. My husband and I have a deep love for our close friend Margie, and we wish her all of the success in the world.

-Judith L. Anker-Nissen
2010

Chapter One

As I awakened, a sensation of being lost and utterly confused engulfed me. Adding further to my distress, I had the unpleasant feeling that I was lying on top of my own body waste.

Panicking, I pounded the mattress beneath me as I slowly edged my body towards the side of the bed. Not being fully aware of where I was or what I was doing, I moved too far and ending up slipping from the mattress and crashing to the floor.

Desperate for help, I reached out my right hand and knocked on everything near me, testing for the feel of a telephone or a buzzer, anything that I could use to summon someone to lift me out of this confusion.

My panic intensified until finally my hand connected with a telephone. Frantically, I pressed on buttons until at last someone answered.

"I need help. Send the management." I rasped into the telephone in as steady a voice as I could muster. "Send security".

Fumbling, I attempted to replace the receiver into its cradle. Under the haze of the anesthesia I missed and the entire contraption crashed to the floor.

A few minutes later, a knock sounded at the door. I grabbed onto whatever I could as I tried to steady myself. Although I was now able to open my eyes a little bit wider, everything remained blurry.

Normally I would have been embarrassed to be seen in such a state, but I was too disoriented to feel much of anything besides confusion and a rising fear.

With great effort, I made my way to the door. Upon opening it I was greeted by a woman who identified herself as the manager. Beside her stood a tall African American man with a muscular build.

Grasping what I could from recent obscure memory, I told them, "A nurse was here. She came from the surgeon's facility. I think I have been over-medicated."

As I spoke, I felt lethargic. I was in severe pain and experiencing nausea. I was also emotionally frail and above all, terribly frightened. I stopped speaking and allowed my eyes to wander over the room. Various items were strewn about that indicated that someone other than me had recently been there.

On the floor lay a satchel that was large enough to pack clothes in. Other pieces of luggage that I knew weren't mine were also lying about. I lacked absolutely any idea of where these items might have come from.

The only thing I knew for certain was that a short time earlier someone other than these managers had been with me in this room.

"Where is this person now?" the manager asked. "Where is the nurse?"

"I have no idea. All I can tell you for sure is that I don't want this individual back in this room."

"Mrs. Shepherd, could you please describe her?"

The only memory I had of a nurse was the one from Dr. Aronowitz's overnight recovery facility. Her name was Kita Stovall.

I stumbled through my mind as I tried to recall as many physical traits about her as possible. However, the confusion was too strong. The details I was able to give were few. "She was African American, a few inches shorter than me. She had dark hair, and that's all I can remember."

About this time, I saw my reflection in a dresser mirror in the hotel room's living quarters. My face was still swollen from surgery. My matted, bleached blonde hair made me look as if I had not bathed in many days.

I could feel the drain tubes behind my ears, still left in my body from the operation. The sensations of being physically sick and disoriented remained strong.

Although I had managed to give some information to the manager, I felt many blind spots, details that I couldn't quite grasp.

"We want to be as helpful as humanly possible," the manager said, adding that she was concerned for me. "Please feel free to call us if you obtain more information about the nurse. If there is anything specific you would like us to do to help, just let us know."

The pair left after about ten minutes. Judging by the angle of the sun streaming through the window of the Crowne Plaza Beverly Hills hotel room, it must have been mid-morning.

Suddenly I realized that other than the manager referring to me as "Mrs. Shepherd," I had very little idea of who I was, beginning from the time I had awakened that morning after regaining consciousness from whatever pharmaceuticals I had been given.

During the first several hours after the manager left, I intermittently experienced sensations of sleepiness, a dull, lethargic feeling as if I had just awakened from anesthesia.

I noted various other items strewn about the room that were not mine. On the floor I spotted a business card. When I picked it up I saw that it contained contact information for Kita Stovall.

Sitting down in the closest chair, I tried to remember why I would have required the services of a registered nurse. The business card listed Cedar-Sinai Medical Center in Los Angeles. Slowly, I began to remember going there for a face-lift and reconstruction surgery on my breast.

As the fog in my mind gradually lifted, I was able to recall specific details, although my mind remained blank when it came to most vital information. Increasingly concerned, I picked up the phone again. My vision had by this time improved slightly although other painful symptoms remained.

"Could you please come to my room?" I asked to whoever answered the hotel's office phone. "There are a number of this other person's personal items left about. I would like you to come get them as I do not recognize them."

"I will arrange for that," the front desk clerk said.

"I will make every effort to have them outside the door, so that you can get them. And I would like you to stop this person from coming up to my room again."

I gave the description of the items to the best of my ability, adding that it would take me a few minutes to get them out of my room. I was hoping to avoid any embarrassing situations and didn't want anyone whether it be a bellman or a clerk to see what I looked like, wearing this nightgown which was soiled by my bodily waste.

I then gave as concise a description of the nurse as possible, so that hotel personnel could stop her in the ground-floor entrance area. Right after this conversation ended, I struggled as I put all my energy into getting those items outside my room and into the hallway.

Chapter Two

Late that morning, the telephone rang. Slowly, I managed to pick up the receiver.

"Miss Shepherd, this is Kita Stovall, your nurse," a voice said in monotone. "My stuff is down here in the lobby. Why? What is going on?"

Instantly I felt a spurt of rage that energized me enough to summon indignation. "That's my question to you! Don't you come up here! Don't you surface in my life! I don't know who you are!"

"But you hired me." the voice protested.

"I didn't hire you, and I don't even know who you are." Despite how terribly I was feeling, the anger I felt towards this person was overwhelming any feeling of weakness that I might have had at that moment.

"I'm from Dr. Aronowitz's office."

"Fine, I still didn't hire you, and I'll call them, too. I'm sicker than hell, and you can go to hell," I said, slamming the phone.

Within the hour, hotel personnel informed me that they had stopped the woman, and given her belongings to her before she left. If I had been completely together mentally at the time when I requested that her items be removed from my room, I would have as well instructed the hotel employees to call the police and have officers arrest her when she appeared in the lobby.

At this point, as my mind was still not functioning at full capacity, I had not been able to clearly recall my identity. After hearing various people call me "Ms. Shepherd," I started searching in my for any clue as to who I might be. The notion of having been drugged or abducted still had not crossed my mind.

I sat for what seemed like an eternity, unable to totally put the pieces together. I noted the tightness I felt around my neck, face and breasts. Gradually, through the remainder of that day, I began to realize how Dr. Aronowitz fit in to the picture as I started to recall that I had visited Los Angeles on two previous occasions to be examined in preparation for surgery.

I also realized that my hair remained matted because of drainage including blood from incisions behind my ears.

Chapter Three

I grew up in a family of low-income earners. Until my second birthday, my mother, Georgia LaRue Thornsberry, a native of Castle Gate, Utah, a coal-mining town, worked as a laborer in the orange groves of North-Central Florida near Orlando. She picked fruit and planted small fruit trees.

Needless to say, fun family activities were rare during my early childhood, as my mother and her family lacked spending money. We survived thanks to their hard-working perseverance and positive attitudes. On my mother's side of the family, our heritage was a mixture of French, Scottish, and American Indian. My maternal grandmother had lived on an Indian reservation.

The majority of my family members were Mormon, although I have no memory of them practicing the faith as I was growing up. I believe my mother's parents, Frank and Lola Thomas, worshiped through the church, but my mother never did. When she was a small child, my mother's family had moved to the Ocoee area of North Central Florida from Utah.

I have no early childhood memories of Bill Thornsberry, my biological father. It not until my teens that relatives told me that shortly after my second birthday Bill had left my mother for another woman.

At 5-foot-4-inches tall, my mother was blessed with natural auburn hair, brown eyes, a creamy complexion, and a proportioned and womanly body. Her bubbly, infectious personality was reflected in her healthy, vivacious aura. She had a keen mind, and a kind, hard-working demeanor.

Her temperament and mine did not coincide. However, as I reflect back it seems to me that I was very savvy about certain things. As a toddler and during my early childhood, I was not ready yet to learn them. These elements would emerge later and combine quite nicely with the drive my mother gave me to succeed

My mother had a lot of talent in many areas. However, her skills and personal attributes were unlike the characteristics that I acquired as the years passed. This is where we differed. In contrast to my personality, Mother lacked the guidance or belief that she could accomplish anything she wanted if she struggled to achieve her goals.

Nevertheless, there is one word that describes a primary attribute my mother instilled in me for which I am still grateful to this day and that is, tenacity.

Mother never excelled in her professional endeavors, until she had reached her late thirties and early forties which turned out to be far too close to the end of her life. To this day, though, I am grateful for the dogged, 'never-say-die' attitude that I inherited from her.

During her own childhood, my mother's life had been very structured. In those times, if you hailed from a family with money, the attitude was, "Well, of course you can do that." By contrast, the general public attitude was that people from poor families could never acquire money or achieve financial success in their own right.

When I was a toddler we lived in Alamonte Springs. At the time it was a horse-town or cow-town filled with many well-known orange production companies. Many of the business and job opportunities available in Alamonte Springs today were not possible in the late 1940s and early 1950s.

I fondly remember the old-fashioned town square located in the heart of the community, embossed with an early 1900s-style courthouse and rickety movie theater. A big splurge was a trip to the ice cream shop or a stroll downtown to watch old-fashioned hot-rods cruising by, relics from my mother's era.

During my early years, my mother's parents initially worked picking oranges. However, my Grandmother Lola studied and became a dietary consultant at Orlando State Hospital, and my Grandpa Frank eventually started working as a carpenter on U.S. military ships at a Navy Base near Pensacola, and as a private carpenter in the building of custom homes.

Beginning from the time I learned to walk, I was definitely Grandpa Frank's little girl the only female child in my family for the past 17 years. My mother, my brother, Bill Junior, who was 18 months younger than I, and myself lived with my Grandma Lola and Grandpa Frank in a small house in Alamonte Springs.

When I was two we moved with my grandparents to the colony of Ocoee just 12 miles from Orlando. Grandpa used his carpentry talents for remodeling and add-ons, making life a lot more comfortable for our entire family.

Ocoee was quite small. If you blinked when driving through it, you stood a high chance of missing it. This was precisely the type of place that many Americans wished existed more often today. For recreation, I shared a bicycle or a tricycle with my brother, until I was finally given a bike of my own.

As a little tow-headed girl with natural curls, I tanned very easily. My mother would dress me in a pair of shorts, and out the door I would go. I relished making mud pies or playing catch in the alleyway behind our home, just up the street from the heart of Ocoee.

My stepfather, Arthur Graham Gustin, whom I still know as my daddy to this day, re-entered my mother's life during that period. It was not until later years that I discovered they had been high school sweethearts in Alamonte Springs. Immediately after graduation Arthur had entered the Air Force.

Before daddy returned to her life, mother had been briefly married to my biological father. Daddy and my mother rekindled their relationship almost immediately after his return from military service.

Everyone called me by my birth name, Margaret, until I entered school, when I started, by my own choice, going by Margie. I suppose the adults would have described me as tenacious at anything I did, a little go-getter. For as long as I can remember words or phrases such as "no," or "it can't be done" did not have any place in my heart.

My Grandma Lola remained very artistic, enjoying crochet and knitting, while my mother preferred sewing. They both loved cooking, and I failed at all of those. However, I think my artistic abilities really began to shine later.

Looking back, I would say that no one other than me could have predicted the tremendous success I would later achieve in business, and of the tragedy involving a nurse that would wipe out the bulk of my fortune as an adult.

Chapter Four

"Margie, are you okay?" a caller asked me about 12 hours after I awakened in my hotel room. It was Judi, a friend of mine from Reno, Nevada.

"I don't know, Jude." I answered truthfully.

I explained to her what I remembered.

Judi said that she had telephoned for me several times during the period when the nurse was in my hotel room. On the first two phone calls, Judi said, the nurse refused to pass the phone to me, telling my friend that "Ms. Shepherd is in no shape to talk."

However, Judi also had called my hotel room on Sept. 2, 2005, the night before I awakened and summoned help. On that occasion, Judi said, the nurse apparently held the phone to my ear. I did not remember that incident at all.

"You were making no sense in your speech," Judi said. "The nurse told me, 'I've just medicated Mrs. Shepherd.'"

I respected everything Judi told me, not only because she is my friend, but also because for fifteen years, she had been an employee of the Florida State Narcotics Bureau. Now a highly accredited employee with a similar position for the state of Nevada, she has been trained to detect when someone is on strong amounts of narcotics.

Unable to sit, I lay on the bed during the last half of our ninety minute phone conversation. Judi made consistent attempts to trigger my memory. She could tell that I was neither physically nor emotionally myself. As we spoke, the maid service came to freshen the room.

"I'm afraid that something very bad has happened to you," Judi said.

It was not until later that I realized that at this time Judi was trying to minimize to me her level of concern, so as not to alarm me.

She began quizzing me as she would have done for anyone whom she suspected had been overly medicated. At this time, I did not have any of the various medications for my long-term health challenges as part of the post-surgery recovery process.

"Margie, you were only supposed to be down there for three to five days," Judi said. "How do you feel about getting on an airplane? Would the doctor let you travel?"

"I don't know. I'm going to call the doctor's office tomorrow," I said, noting that by now it was dark outside. I knew that there would not be anyone at the physician's office at such a late hour.

Judi and I agreed to talk again the next day, and needless to say, I felt glad to have such a good friend.

After we hung up, I managed to make my way to the bathroom. I removed a fresh pair of pajamas from my suitcase, which was open. My movements remained very lethargic and confusion was still very much present. It was extremely difficult to get into the bathtub to turn on the shower.

Instead, I sat on the commode with the lid down, leaned over the sink, pulled up the lever to close the sink off, and turned on the cold water. Picking up a washcloth I doused it and tried to wash my legs and stomach.

It certainly did not amount to a thorough bathing attempt. I just wanted to do get the excrement and urine off and discard the clothes, a horrible reminder of the nurse.

Later in the evening, several other acquaintances, including a Reno couple, Deanna and Max, phoned me to express their concern.

Throughout the day, I had been crying off as well as during my conversations with the hotel managers and Judi. In each instance, I had tried to respond as articulately as I could, stumbling as I tried to think out my next move.

I fail to recall whether I was able to eat that day, which ended as I, physically incapable of doing anything more and unable to focus on the appropriate people to call, cried myself to sleep.

Chapter Five

When I was about three years old going on four, my mother's new husband moved her, my brother and me more than four hundred miles away to an out-of-the-way place near Miami in Southern Florida. Many enjoyable hours were spent on the beach, where I splashed happily into the ocean.

At one point, I got caught in a wave, . Fortunately, my mother was right there. She reached down and grabbed me by the hair, pulling me up as my mouth filled with the salty water.

Daddy worked for a swimming pool installation company, occasionally at homes of celebrities included famed comedian Red Skelton. He earned a respectable income, enabling us mother to buy our first house. Daddy's work kept him in another area much of the time, but he always came home on weekends.

Mother enjoyed being a housewife and was able to do so comfortably as daddy earned enough money to support us all. In the early 1950s, when I was five, Mother gave birth to my youngest brother, Bobby.. By that time we had moved to Brandon in the Tampa Bay Area, where daddy had landed a good part-time job as a driver for the Safeway store chain.

In time, the company's managers promoted him to a full-time position as a milk driver, delivering dairy products and eggs to various Safeway stores. At this point, my mother was not considered to be very highly qualified as she had never finished high school. She did her best to earn as much money as possible, working part-time at Louie's Restaurant in Pinellas Park, a better- than-average diner.

Mother realized that in order to obtain a position with improved hours she needed to earn a high school diploma. Her decision made, she attended class while maintaining her job. She and daddy rotated their shifts so that there was always someone at home to care for the children. Within several years, my mom had earned her high school degrees.

My mother had also applied to work for Safeway, deemed a good employer in those days because of its adequate pay and company's benefits that included health insurance. As a married couple, both working for the same company, they could interchange benefits in certain areas in order to ensure our family was covered and protected at all times.

When I was in my mid-teens, my mother was hired by Safeway. At that time, we lived on Colusa Street in Brandon Valley. Track homes were very popular. My parents bought one that needed a little bit of work, and they fixed it up. Like my Grandpa Frank, daddy was very handy at building things.

Daddy built a wishing well, flower pots, fences, and other such amenities that enhanced the appearance of the house and increased its value. By this point, we children were old enough for my parents to assign us household chores.

Back in Ocoee, my grandparents remained in the house that Grandpa Frank had refurbished. Grandma Lola continued working for the Orlando State Hospital, and Grandpa still liked carpentry work.

We visited them often, spending delightful days that will remain forever in my memory.

Down the alley-way, right across the main street— which was a two-lane highway sat an old, boarded-up hotel owned by a man who fenced off the property. A palomino horse ran loose inside that area. While living in Brandon, every time we visited my grandparents in Ocoee, I would casually say "Oh, I have to go out." I would then disappear down the alley, across the road, and under the fence. holding some apples or other treats which I would then feed to the horse.

Once there I would step up on part of a tree trunk. The horse would follow me around because it wanted more apples, sugar, chocolate chip cookies, or whatever I could sneak out of my grandma's pantry. Whether a horse should have chocolate chip cookies, I couldn't tell you. But that horse ate anything and everything I gave it.

When the horse came up to the tree trunk, I would grab its mane. Eventually, the horse began to recognize me and whenever I visited, would immediately start walking over to me.

As soon as the horse reached me, wanting its treat, it would begin to nudge my arms.

One day, after many days of following this routine, I grabbed the horse's mane and climbed up from a chopped-off area of the tree trunk onto its bare back. Sliding my head and stomach onto the horse, I tried to squeeze my little leg over it. It was not easy as the horse was very rounded in comparison to my small size.

From that day forward, every time I visited the horse, I rode it around the property. I was usually dressed in a t-shirt and shorts. My curly hair would billow out slightly in the gentle wind as the horse increased its pace to a gallop. Sheer pleasure formed a smile on my face and I often found myself laughing with the very joy of the moment. ,I loved the animal dearly and treasured the simple pleasure the rides brought to me. These happy visits continued for several years.

I truly felt that that no-one knew of these visits, that I had a precious secret. The very notion of hiding it from everybody delighted me. "Boy, not only do I think this is the best time in the whole world," I remember thinking to myself. "But it's my secret. And I did it all by myself, and nobody has said to me that I can't do it."

To be sure, nobody ever told me "you're going to make it one day," or "you have great talent," or "you're beautiful," or "isn't she cute." No such statements had ever been uttered, for this would not have been typical of the background from which I hailed.

Even though I believed that I would never get caught, it was inevitable that I finally did. One day the man who owned the horse and the property drove up in his rickety old truck. He saw me riding his horse.

"Little girl! Little girl! What are you doing?" he hollered.

Startled, I looked around and muttered to myself, "Oh, oh, who's that?"

I looked at the man for what seemed like an eternity and finally told him: "I'm riding the horse."

"You're not supposed to ride that horse. That horse isn't safe."

Unable to figure out what he meant, since the horse had never seemed to pose any danger to me, I got off the animal that I loved so dearly and stood by it, gently patting its side.

"Little girl, I don't want you to come back here again, or else I'm going to tell your parents."

On that particular day, I went through the motions of following this man's orders. However, I was very determined and his admonitions failed to stop me. On subsequent visits to Grandma's house I simply found areas of his property that were out of sight.

It was not so much that I was deliberately being mischievous or disobedient. It was just that in my mind, the word "no" simply did not exist. For me, the only appropriate term was and still is "we'll find a better way." In fact, I felt that riding this horse and loving it so much was truly one of the first major accomplishments I had ever achieved.

In the end, I managed to keep my rides secret. The fact was that, the horse liked me. If the horse avoided being receptive with people in general, then perhaps my success with the animal stemmed from my approach or maybe something about me. I never figured it out completely until many years later.

One day, when I was about 13, while visiting Grandma's, I made my usual run up the alley toward the old hotel property. When I arrived the horse was nowhere in sight. I crawled under the fence and walked all the way around the dilapidated building with its broken or boarded-up windows.

"Hello!" I hollered, trying to catch the horse's attention. "Hello!"

I failed to find the animal and it did not appear. At that point, I did not know much about horses, even whether it was a mare or gelding. All I knew for sure was that it had four legs, it was a horse, and I liked riding it because it meant I was succeeding at something.

From that point forward, the projects that I would set out for myself gradually and steadily became a little larger with each progressive accomplishment. I also decided to buy my own horse,— to achieve whatever I wanted in life, and to never let anyone rob me of the happiness that I deserved.

Chapter Six

Early on the morning of September 4, 2005, after I had awakened from a drug-induced stupor, I received a call from the limousine driver who had driven me each time I had come to Los Angeles to prepare for my recent surgery. The chauffeur was employed by Triangle Limousine, a company that offered limo service to the hotel.

"Mrs. Shepherd, this is Mark Templeton, your driver," he said. "Do you know that you were taken to Wells Fargo Bank, and that you were taken shopping at Louis Vuitton® in Beverly Hills?"

"No." I truly had no recollection of such happenings.

"You were, and I tried to talk to the nurse who was with you. You were in no shape to go anywhere."

Stunned, I listened as Mark explained that both he and George Pasco, another driver from the same company, had been very concerned about my well being.

"Mrs. Shepherd, we've been worried that the nurse was taking advantage of you. Do you recall any expenses you paid to the nurse?" Although he spoke gently, I could hear the concern in his voice.

"No, I don't remember that," I said, honestly still unable to recall any of what he was telling me. "Could you hold on?"

"Okay."

While Mark waited on the line, despite the dull feeling I had in my body from the medication, I forced myself over to where my purse was in the hotel room, .I needed to retrieve both my checkbook and my pocketbook. Right away, I spotted a couple entries in my checkbook register that I knew nothing about. They were handwritten records of one check for nineteen thousand dollars to Kita Stovall, and a three thousand three hundred dollar check to a medical facility, the name of which I failed to recognize. Even more than I had the previous day, I realized that, indeed, something very wrong had transpired.

Before returning to the phone, I picked up my pocketbook and my 9-year-old Louis Vuitton® purse, a gift from my late husband. Even though it had a broken zipper, I kept it for sentimental reasons.

"Mark, it's written here in my checkbook register, something about a nursing care service for three thousand three hundred dollars," I said. "And there's a nineteen thousand dollar check to a person named Kita Stovall. ... I thought I had made arrangements to have a private nurse meet me at the hotel. But I don't know where this person came from."

Expressing deep concern, Mark explained that on Sept.ember 1, 2005, the morning after the scheduled surgery, he had driven his limo to the entrance of a medical building— which was Cedars-Sinai Medical Towers. He had dropped me off there the previous day.

"My memory of you picking me up is very sketchy," I told him. "I don't have any recollection of going to the bank. I really don't have any idea of what this three thousand three hundred dollars was for, or even the nineteen thousand dollars."

"Well, the nurse was very controlling," Mark said. "She had called me the day of your medical procedure. During that call, she demanded that I bring six hundred dollars to her, for you to use as spending money."

Mark explained that before 6 o'clock on the morning of my release from the medical facility he had driven me and the nurse back to my hotel from there. He said the nurse had told him to return to the hotel to pick the two of us up at 11 o'clock that morning to take us to Wells Fargo Bank.

From there, Mark said, he was directed to take the nurse to a bank where I assume she had an account.

"Mark, I need to go to Wells Fargo this morning, because there's also an entry here to Kita Stovall for nineteen thousand dollars," I said. "Are you available to drive me there?"

"Yes, by all means, I'll try to make myself available, Mrs. Shepherd."

"I can't go back to the bank the way I look right now," I said, concerned that my hair was still matted with drainage of blood and other body fluids from the surgery. "I will see if I can make an appointment with a beauty shop close by."

After chatting with Mark I called the hotel front desk and asked if someone could recommend a beauty shop. It seemed to take me forever to put on something a little more respectable than my pajamas. The front desk called to tell me the hotel had made an appointment for me in ninety minutes at a salon about a mile and a half away.

I asked the clerk to contact Mark to see if he was available to drive me to the salon at the scheduled time, and then from there to Wells Fargo. Within minutes, the clerk called back to confirm with the availability of the chauffeur.

Shortly afterward, prior to Mark picking me up for the salon appointment, I phoned the office of Dr. Aronowitz, the plastic surgeon. A receptionist informed me that he was in surgery. I then asked to speak with JoAnn, the young woman at the office who had initially prepared my enrollment form to arrange for surgery.

"Does Dr. Aronowitz have a nurse by the name of Kita Stovall?" I asked her.

"Yes, Kita works part-time, and she works with a lot of the patients after surgery in the overnight facility at the doctor's compartment. On the day you had your surgery, Kita was in the night-time facility, our patients' recuperation area."

"Okay, but this is what has happened," I said, before explaining how I had awakened from what I thought was a period of over-medication. I told JoAnn that I had no knowledge of where Kita Stovall had come from,. I then described to her the mysterious checkbook entries, adding that items were missing from my purse.

The process of describing these details, prompted me to remember other things. I was also able to tell JoAnn that the nurse had kept repeating to me: "Don't tell Dr. Aronowitz."

Without hesitation, JoAnn admitted to me that she was completely shocked by what I had just related to her: "Mrs. Shepherd," she said, "when the doctor gets out of surgery, I will tell him everything. He'll probably call you."

Considering the circumstances, I would say that this conversation ended on a cordial note. I then spent several minutes checking my appearance before the limo driver was to arrive. I felt much better now that I was wearing loose slacks, a comfortable top, and flat shoes.

As I exited the elevator to the hotel lobby, I spotted Mark standing at the hotel entrance. Moving slowly, I made my way across the short distance to the door. Mark greeted me, then assisted me to the car.

"How are you, Mrs. Shepherd?" he asked.

"Not well," I said, . My eyesight was still blurry so I was quite glad that at least I was able to recognize him.

Mark was a native of Romania, as were the majority of limo drivers who served that hotel at the time. A very striking man, in terms of his looks and manner of, dress, he was also very kind and a gentleman. His face, narrowing down to his chin which reminded me in form of the letter "V,", was both elegant and masculine.

At all times, the chauffeur kept his hair very well styled. He was meticulously groomed, impeccable in appearance. To his credit, he always wore a well-pressed, fashionable three-piece suit with a white shirt. His ties were of various colors and patterns, and always perfectly matched to his suit. The smart dress shoes he favored were always well-polished.

Always a consummate professional, he held himself and walked with a sense of obvious dignity, . He was the type of person that most people would feel compelled to want to know.

Mark took his time explaining to me what had happened. From his expressions I could see that he felt my appearance was different from what he was used to seeing in me. He recognized and acknowledged that I did not look well and was mentally disoriented. Once again, from the beginning, he recounted the events from several days earlier.

"The nurse called me on the day of your surgical procedures— to tell me what time I should pick you up the next morning," he said. "That call came from Kita Stovall, and as I told you this morning, she told me to bring six hundred dollars to her."

At this point, I feel it is essential for me to stress that at all times before and immediately after the events, Mark was extremely professional in all his dealings with me. His care of me has always been of the highest level. We had absolutely no connection between each other as family members or in personal involvement other than business.

Thus, I believed— then and continue to fully believe— now Mark's statements. His assertions about Kita Stovall's request for six hundred dollars left me perplexed, especially given that she had done so before the surgical procedures.

While en route to the salon, Mark went into more detail than he had on the phone.

"That morning, Mrs. Shepherd, you were all bandaged up, and you were in your pajamas," he said. "It was like you were a completely different person from the woman I had known."

Learning the details of Kita Stovall's behavior, I felt violated and taken advantage of but very fortunate to have him as a driver. I felt grateful that he had tried to intervene with the woman and to interact with me.

Before long we arrived at the salon. Upon entering I gave the receptionist my name. At this point, however, I still was not functioning at full capacity. Everything around me, along with my own thought process and movements, seemed to progress in super-slow motion.

It was clear from the expression on the face of , the salon professional that she realized I was not fully in control of my actions or movements. Her expression remained one of concern as she questioned me as to what I wanted done with my hair.

During the forty-five minutes that it took to wash and style my hair, Mark remained outside. I explained to the technician that the incisions and drainage at the back of my head were the result of recent reconstructive surgery.

After leaving the salon, Mark drove me back to the branch of the Wells Fargo Bank where he had taken me and Kita Stovall at her direction on the morning of my release from the medical facility. This time, I walked inside alone while Mark waited in the limo.

After hearing my explanation about the two checks that I had not in full conscience or willingly written, clerks at the teller window informed me that I would have to speak to Armita and asked her to come to the counter. When the young woman arrived, I identified myself and related to her what I remembered.

Without hesitation, Armita became very antagonistic, insisting that I had known what I was doing, . She continued by telling me that I had written the check for nineteen thousand dollars, and stated in a very cold-hearted tone: "Mrs. Shepherd, you're going to have to pay."

"Is there another bank manager, or general manager, or somebody that ranks above you?" I asked.

"I'm the only one on duty, and there is nobody else here for you to talk to." she replied defensively.

Disappointed at Armita's reaction, I asked for her name, and phone number. I offered my home number, although it did not occur to me at the time that they already had that information in their system. I was trying very hard to put all the pieces together.

"I didn't know anything about this," I said to Armita. "I didn't even know that I was here. And I don't know that individual who wrote the checks. I have no intention of paying this bank nineteen thousand dollars. I understand by looking in my register that she also wrote one for three thousand three hundred dollars, but it was for a nursing facility. I don't even know where that is."

After about twenty , the futility of the situation was clear. I was receiving no sign of sympathy from this bank executive, whom I felt was refusing to acknowledge the seriousness of the situation. I turned around and walked out of the building—. My state of total fear and confusion, was further exacerbated by sensations of sickness. One thing of what I was certain was that I had never written those checks, I failed to understand why Armita so adamantly insisted otherwise.

Seated back in the limo, I related to Mark what had happened: "They say that I knew exactly what I was doing the other day when you took the two of us to the bank." I told him. "But I don't remember a thing."

"Mrs. Shepherd, you were really sick, and that nurse took advantage of you," he responded, before giving me more details. "Kita Stovall and her husband had engaged our limo services. They went to a high-end Beverly Hills restaurant, where they bought a lot of food."

"I didn't give the woman permission to do that, and I never would have done so." I insisted. I was very clear on that.

Mark further told me that on the night of the restaurant visit, the couple had been driven by George, his associate. "Mrs. Shepherd,

George told me that the two had left the restaurant holding bags of food."

As it turned out, the pair had charged just over five hundred dollars for that night's limo services to my American Express card, and they had used the same card to pay three hundred and fifty dollars for dinner.

Hearing these details, my feelings of being violated intensified. Overwhelmed, I tried to figure out what my next move should be. Given that the information that had just been transmitted to me had further intensified the shock of the situation, I was unable to conclude that calling my attorney and the police would have been a wise and logical move.

Chapter Seven

One day , when I was 12 years old, my parents stayed home from work, telling me and my brother, Bill Junior, "We all have an appointment. And we all have to go."

"Okay, fine," I said, without realizing the impact of the events that were about to take place. We arrived at the courthouse where I learned that for many years my daddy and mother had not been receiving child support from my biological father.

My parents had kept track of these missed payments. Finally, they contacted Bill Thornsberry through legal counsel. The lawyers informed him of the amount owed and presented him with a due date. He made no effort to pay.

As a result, my parents made arrangements to have daddy adopt Bill Junior and I. At that time, I had no concept of what was happening, and I thought it really odd that we were in a courtroom.

A man who was a complete stranger to me was sitting up on a pedestal. He started asking me about my daddy and mother, and then asked my brother similar questions. Bill and I answered everything he asked before leaving with our parents. From that point on, I started using the surname Gustin in school, although I never received a full explanation from my parents as to what had just happened.

During the years I was growing up, I still had little concept of my own tremendous drive and tenacity. Just after my 16th birthday, as had most of my classmates, I obtained a driver's license. My relatives suggested that I drive my daddy's Corvair. One day, while attending physical education class in high school, I was given the message that I was to return home immediately.

I collected my belongings, my books and homework, and drove home. When I arrived at the house, I noticed my mother standing at the kitchen window. She was rinsing something in sink. When I entered through the door, I noticed that, my daddy was sitting in a chair to my left, and a stranger was sitting in a chair directly in front of me.

"Margaret, I would like you to meet your father," my mother said, motioning toward the stranger. "This is Bill Thornsberry."

I stood motionless staring at the man, shocked beyond belief. My family had never mentioned any other father to me. The reality of what I had just been told hit me hard, as if someone had thrown a bucket of ice water over my head. I looked at mother, and then moved my gaze toward the stranger. I took about four steps backward while holding my arm out which I immediately wrapped around my daddy's neck.

"He's not my father," I said. "This is my daddy. This is my daddy."

I stood there and looked at Bill Thornsberry, as he gave me a blank stare. At that time, I failed to realize that there had been an ulterior motive in arranging for me to meet this person, this stranger, who was really, as I now knew, my biological father..

Chapter Eight

While driving me back to the hotel from the bank after I had just received the horrific news, Mark, must have noticed that I had become even more distressed and confused than I had been previously.

Immediately upon my return to the hotel, I asked the front desk clerks to remove my name from the registry.

"I want to be listed as a Jane Doe, for the remainder of my stay here" I told them. My purpose for this was to prevent Kita Stovall from slipping past hotel personnel and getting to my living quarters.

To the facility's credit they honored my request without asking any questions. It was my fourth day after surgery, and I remained frightened and worried. As I received more information about what had happened, my concerns gradually intensified.

Having not eaten since awakening the day before, I ordered food from room service. Barely able to swallow I struggled to eat the items delivered. However, I soon vomited into the toilet. For the remainder of that afternoon and during the next several days, I was only able to ingest liquids.

My plight was compounded by a severe digestive disorder that has plagued me for forty years throughout my adult life, beginning at age 20 when I contracted colon cancer. Stress coupled with food could cause flare-ups that resulted in vomiting. At times I entered a phase when swallowing solid foods was simply impossible.

When such a flare-up occurs, it is essential for people with these types of severe digestive disorders to eat solids in order to prompt their systems into functioning again. When unable to eat solids, people with this condition should next try liquids such as broth, ice tea or clear sodas, slowly graduating to more solid foods such as Jell-O®.

To this day, I remain convinced that my chronic health problems, coupled with having been over-medicated, exacerbated the confusion and physical symptoms of sickness I was experiencing. This combination of circumstances also had the consequence of rendering me unable to make rational decisions during the first several days after I had awakened.

Already very fragile, my physical state became weaker. Unable to eat solids, I found it difficult to maintain my already, at 5 foot five inches tall, lean 125-pound frame. In keeping with standard procedure, medical personnel had prohibited me from eating on the day of the surgery, and I could not recall having eaten solids since then.

Slowly sipping water, I sat alone in my hotel room during the first few hours after my return. I am unsure at this point of the exact time that my hotel room phone rang, but I believe it probably was that afternoon.

"Hello, Mrs. Shepherd?"

"Yes, Dr. Aronowitz?" I recognized his voice.

"I'm returning your call. I received your message concerning some disturbing details. What happened? I can't believe this. I am shocked."

"You're shocked?" I said. Seizing this opportunity I informed the doctor of the listings in my bank account registry, and what had transpired during my visit to the bank when I had disputed writing the two checks. I pointed out to him that the three thousand three hundred dollar check to a nursing service was listed as having been written on August 31, the day of surgery, a date when I could not possibly have posted such a document.

"Dr. Aronowitz, this should not have happened," I said. "This is a total violation of me as a woman, of me putting my trust in you, and of me putting my trust in your staff. I underwent over even and a half hours of surgery."

I then told him the basic details of what I remembered.

"Margie, I'll look into this." he promised.

"Okay," I said, unable to stop crying.

Margie Shepherd

"I would like to see you again in my office. It's not a good idea for you to try to get on an airplane at this time. As I recall, Mrs. Shepherd, you were only supposed to be in Los Angeles for three to five days."

As our conversation ended, I had no way of knowing that some of my most difficult days were still ahead of me.

Chapter Nine

Throughout my childhood and teen years, I was intrigued by horses and held a passion for them. When I was about thirteen, I started saving the money I made babysitting in the hopes of one day buying my own horse. I considered myself advanced for my years , and a fully responsible individual.

I would have been happy to have a horse of any kind, and soon became interested in horse shows. At the age of fifteen and a half, shortly after getting my driver's license learner permit, I had saved two hundred dollars, enough to buy a young Morgan mixed gelding quarter-horse.. More money would have been required to buy the higher- caliber of horse that I really wanted.

Even so, I loved my horse and gave him the care and attention that I could. I gave him the name Beau-K, pronounced "bouquet," after discover him eating flowers.

At the time, I considered my interaction with this horse as a true relationship, which brings to mind the meaning of the word "beau.". I went daily to feed and brush him. Only something life-threatening would have prevented me from attending to that horse.

Shortly after I purchased the horse, my daddy found a place to board him in nearby Plant City. My horse was young, and this told me that he could still be properly trained. Even though I lacked the skills to train him, I did the best that I could. As soon as I turned sixteen, I received my driver's license. I could now drive myself to Plant City without having to depend on my parents for transportation.

The boarding stable was not in the best of condition. It featured a typical dirt arena and substandard fencing, . It was so old that it seemed a sneeze could cause the stall's side panels to fall. On the positive side, however, I obtained gate privileges that enabled me to take my horse out to a swampy, but mostly dry area, behind the facility.

One day, I took the bus to downtown Jacksonville, where I went to a clothing store that had recently added a sportswear department adjacent to its main sales facility. Impressed by my appearance, the store manager hired me as a part-time sales clerk , and as a teen model for its fashion shows. I had naturally curly dark hair and a very well-developed figure, a stunning, attractive physical appearance similar to my mother's.

With management's blessing, I scheduled my work hours to allow me adequate time to care for Beau-K, and still have the opportunity to complete my day's homework.

Unlike formal fashion shows where models wear make-up, these events were informal, and held at non-scheduled times. I wore the latest sportswear, items that would be displayed in the store windows for passers-by to see.

At first the store paid me minimum wage, but after a period of time they told me that I could join the retail clerks union. This gave me a sense of accomplishment, as at age sixteen I was joining the same organization that my mother belonged to as a Safeway checker. Ultimately my mother worked in a booth, where people would go to cash checks.

I had become very protective of certain things in my life, and one of them was my first horse, Beau-K. I had taken some enormous steps with the horse although I was unable to compete in horse shows with him. Whenever necessary, amid my scheduled absences from the horse boarding facility, I made arrangements to have someone feed and care for him.

I made this message very clear to the people I hired. "You avoid mishandling Beau-K, and you do not hurt him, or fool with him."

I saved all my earnings from the store clerk and modeling work and by my seventeenth birthday, was able to buy a second horse. Although my new horse was better, to a certain degree, as far as caliber than Beau-K it was my first horse that truly held my heart.

A young woman who lived and worked at the stables had told me that she would feed Beau-K for me. However, unbeknownst to me, instead of feeding him the food that I had purchased she fed him leftover food containing thorns.

The tainted meal sickened Beau-K for quite a while. . Bloated like a round kitchen table, his body became wracked with severe pain as veterinary expenses mounted to astronomical levels.

As you might imagine, I remained on the lookout for the culprit who had poisoned my animal. Finally one day, I spotted the young woman at the stables.

Without uttering a word of warning, I literally attacked her, first grabbing her by the hair, and then throwing her on the ground. I had never before done anything physical like this.

After knocking the woman down, I jumped on top of her and sat on her chest as I pummeled her face and body non-stop. Shorter than I and a bit older, she possessed a figure which could only be described as dumpy and rather unfeminine.

Coming from a family with money, she wore the best, most expensive boots available and clothes matching the colors of her horse's stall. Her horse, a nice-looking mare, whose saddle, chest harness, and bridle were trimmed with silver, had just recently delivered a foal. Some might think that the natural thing for me to do would be to sabotage or harm this young woman's horse, but there was no way I could ever do that. It had not been her horse who hurt my animal. It had been her.

"Don't you ever touch Beau-K again!" I screamed, amazed at myself. Until this point I never knew that I could be so physically strong. It was an exhilarating feeling to get even with someone for hurting something that I loved so dearly. That animal was my friend, my beau, and my companion. I could always go and talk to my horse. He was not going to tell anyone my secrets and that was a good feeling.

I had learned early on in life that people who wrong you should not escape having to face justice. Whenever such serious matters have risen since then, I have reacted with the same intensity. I have never allowed anyone to get away with hurting me .However, after that first incident in which I physically attacked the woman, I have used legal means to exact justice on others rather than resorting to violence.

It is this sense of justice and these strong ethics that I carried over into my later years, as I vowed that Kita Stovall would never escape whatever legal vengeance I could wreak upon her.

Chapter Ten

Disoriented and struggling to recover from being over-medicated, I remained at the Crowne Plaza Beverly Hills Hotel in Los Angeles for sixteen days, extending what originally had been intended to be a three to five day stay following my surgery. My original plan had been to fly home to Reno no later than the fifth day after undergoing the surgical procedures.

I remained physically and emotionally sick during my entire time at the hotel. A bouquet of flowers arrived at my room from Dr. Aronowitz. To me, this added insult to injury. From my viewpoint the physician had refused to talk to me in detail when we had spoken by phone.

Each day after awakening, I still felt disoriented. Nine days after the surgery, I tried attempted to contact my attorney, Tina Halliburton, who was handling my personal affairs in San Francisco. A phone receptionist there informed me that she was out of town on a family emergency.

The law firm's administrators referred me to another attorney from the same office, Tom Adamson. When we eventually connected by phone, I explained what had happened to the best of my knowledge.

I remember him as being cordial and very nice over the phone. He called several times during my hotel stay, and asked why I had waited until around the ninth day after surgery to call his office rather than within a few days.

I explained that for at least the first three to four days, I had been in no shape to speak with anyone. In fact, at this point, I was still disoriented and struggling to recover. I told him that I had contacted hotel management as soon as I started emerging from the over-medication. I stressed that for several days after that process began, I remained so physically ill and emotionally distraught that all that concerned me was getting my name off the hotel register for the sake of personal security.

Expressing deep concern, Adamson began calling me daily wanting to know whatever various bits and pieces of the whole incident that I could remember. I was still extremely confused and vague and only able to give small amounts of information. As my memory improved, as able to transmit to him further details.

Within several days, my regular attorney, Halliburton, returned She and Adamson held a conference call with me, in which she expressed her personal concern for my well-being.

"Hon, are you okay?" she asked.

"No, I'm kind of sick."

Although I was later told that during that conversation the attorneys suggested launching a lawsuit against both Dr. Aronowitz and Cedars-Sinai medical center, I have no memory of such statements taking place. I was still very disoriented and certainly in no condition to make those types of decisions.

. The only thing that I felt for certain was that it was the nurse who was at fault.

During the two years following the incident of August 2005, my focus was on bringing the nurse to justice and protecting myself and the doctor against her actions. I had great respect for Dr. Aronowitz and went out of my way to ensure that he was not caught in the line of fire, as it were. To me, the entire incident was an initiative planned and carried out by Kita Stovall.

In a testament to my confused state of mind, Dr. Aronowitz provided an affidavit declaring that at that point in time when I conversed with Halliburton and Adamson, I was still too disoriented to make any positive calls. He outlined my fragile medical condition and stated his shock

at the nurse's behavior and her demands for funds.

I started to make an accounting to the attorneys of what I remembered before going into surgery. Upon hearing these details, they said that they would look into other areas such as surveillance photos from the bank.

At no time during this phone call or individual conversations with these attorneys did I tell them "you are hired by me for this case."

Tina Halliburton had been on my payroll for a year prior to my surgery handling my personal estate affairs.

Adamson specializes in cases of fraud or civil litigation. At least at the time, Halliburton concentrated on other types of cases. Regarding my particular situation, Adamson reported to her.

During the occasions when Adamson, speaking over the phone became exasperated, he would make repetitive statements to me such as: "Well, you didn't contact me until the ninth of September."

On that date, my attorneys issued a request to Wells Fargo Bank to check my signature on the nineteen thousand dollar check. The bank's employees issued a written statement along with a copy of the check, verifying that someone other than me had written the signature. That person was, Kita Stovall.

All through the initial conference call with the attorneys, I remained physically sick and confused. This conditions lasted for nine months following the surgery. I wanted to stay inside my hotel room. I was scared and terribly afraid of being confronted by the nurse.

Would the Kita Stovall try to drug me again? And if so, how?

Chapter Eleven

Shortly after graduating from high school, I was still working at the junior shop for Marlene's Apparel on McDonald Avenue in Plant City, Florida. At that time, the big greatest form of entertainment for teenagers and young adults was to drive up and drown Main Street. This activity was known as "dragging main.".

lOne evening in early fall, I got off duty a little after nine o'clock. I walked out the store and stood on a corner waiting for a the traffic light to change. While I was standing there, a car pulled up, its front and back seat windows rolled down.

"Hi, my name is Marvin," the driver said. "I would like to meet you."

"Oh, okay," I said in a friendly tone. In those days, things were different and such statements by young motorists were not considered potentially dangerous as they are today. For the most part, back then such situations truly just presented a means of meeting somebody.

The turquoise blue-green Impala, that this mysterious young man drove, sported some interesting details including prized chrome wheels. In my mind, this scenario was comparable to the handsome Clark Gable, playing Rhett Butler as he wooed Scarlett O'Hara in Margaret Mitchell's eternal classic Civil War epic novel "Gone With the Wind."

Intrigued, I allowed this twenty-three year-old stranger to take me for a ride. Straight away we hit it off really well. At that time, some people would have questioned the five year difference.

I talked about my horse, Beau-K, and I told Marvin how I had begun working at the clothing store, I said that at age seventeen I had graduated the previous June from high school. Our voices must have sounded like cheery chipmunks as we drove up and down the main street before we stopped to get something to eat.

"I have a yearly party to go to being held by my employer for employees and their families," he said. "I'd like you to go with me."

The thought that kept crossing my mind was that someone really cool had just stopped and wanted to talk to me. Before long, Marvin started calling regularly.

Shortly thereafter, I quit my job, and applied for another position as a file clerk and telephone receptionist at a downtown Tampa office of the Dun & Bradstreet financial firm.

I was hired by the managers, given my own desk, and told me to learn about the company's financial reporting system. Each workday, I took a Greyhound bus to the city. In order to leave by six each morning and arrive at the office by eight, I had to get up at five o'clock. Naturally, the return trips were arduous as well. I felt very grateful whenever Marvin called and arranged to pick me up.

Into the second month after our meeting, Marvin drove me to the middle-class Clearwater home of his married friends. While at the house, I chatted with the wife, Sheila, as the men barbecued hamburgers in the back yard.

"Oh, Marvin really likes you!" Sheila told me. "I've never seen him like this."

"He likes me?" I responded, in a voice that I imagine must have sounded quite young and innocent. "Why would he like me?"

I lacked confidence in relationships, although by this point I had experienced some non-serious teenage-type situations. Up until this point in my life, I had not been romantically active. Rather than showing any interest in boys, I was more interested in my horse and making money. While I thought it was fun to go out on dates, I really lacked any yearning for serious involvement.

Naturally, a lot of the young men my age were experiencing sexual overdrive, but I was just not interested. More than anything, I wanted to make money, become self sufficient, and establish whatever kind of life I would eventually have.

Little did I know that something that was not in my plans was about to occur. As Marvin drove us home from the couple's house, while on the freeway he proposed: "Margie, will you marry me?"

In those days, it was considered the 'chic' thing to do to get married, and have children,. Therefore, what I mistook to be love was actually just a fluttering of the ideal. Truth be told, although my focus in life was elsewhere, I rather liked the idea that someone really wanted me, and I was awestruck by this revelation Marvin was five foot nine inches tall and trim. He had very dark, naturally curly hair. He wore typical attire for the time, Levi® blue jeans and a white, heavy, thick cotton polo-neck T-shirt. I found him quite attractive.

"Yes," I told Marvin. "I'll marry you. I have to ask my father and mother."

That was the typical, old-fashioned way to go about these things.

If I had truly analyzed the situation, I would have realized that I had gone against my own inner nature, However, my newfound affection for him lasted quite awhile. Soon afterward, though, we found ourselves dealing with a large amount of interference from his family. An active young man, Marvin often took me to a cabin his parents owned about an -hour's drive away in the Lake Okeechobee region close to a popular state park. We enjoyed swimming in the lake, and spending time at the cabin which was located up a little side road.

For me, though, these activities were not that great of an experience. They were tainted by having someone else's parents tell me what to do and how to do it. I very much resented their directives.

Marvin hailed from a family of Hillsborough County Fire Department employees. His father worked in the department's equipment room, and his uncle in the company's main firehouse with my fiancé. Gradually, as the months and years passed, Marvin climbed up the ranks within the department.

My parents asked me, "Well, when do you want to get married?"

"In six months or whatever," I said.

"Are you two going to go away and get married, and are you planning on a big wedding?" daddy asked.

"I don't want a huge ceremony." I really was not into that sort of thing.

Hearing this, my parents encouraged me to take a gift from them of ten thousand dollars, a huge amount of money at the time. Daddy suggested, "Why don't you just fly out west to Tarpon Springs, or Reno, or even Las Vegas, and just get married?"

During this period, track homes were sprouting up all over the Brandon region. Following the trend at the time, average working folks like my parents bought what people commonly referred to as "little rentals" from track home developments.

Inspired and determined to make a sound investment, daddy purchased such a home, which he soon sold for a profit. With my mother's help and encouragement, he invested those profits in several similar properties, completing any repairs, remodeling and upgrades himself.

Daddy was a very entrepreneurial, forward-thinking person. My mother and my father both possessed that same quality, but continued to maintained their permanent Safeway jobs in order to keep long-term security.

Without realizing it at the time, their strong work ethic was instilled in me. It became a natural part of me because that was what I observed and that was what I knew. Nonetheless, their investment skills did require polishing.

By caring for Beau-K while working and attending school, I firmly established my this same work ethic which greatly contributed to my success later in life. Ultimately, by the time I had graduated, the Brandon house where we lived was sold as were the other two houses that daddy owned.

As they liquidated some assets, my parents built a home on a previously undeveloped lot featuring a distant view of Plant City. The broad landscape was adorned by horses, cows and a lovely rural area. To access the property, we drove along a narrow road located at the corner of Marvin Court and Plant City Street.

The home that they built was considered nothing less than spectacular at the time, and they had only paid twenty-seven thousand dollars for it. As I graduated from high school, they were moving into the new house.

Daddy had a stronger influence on me than my mother did. In my mind, the age-old phrase describes them perfectly: "He was the gun, and my mother was the bullet."

Although they would think up strategies both individually and together, they would execute their plans through her. As the years passed, I could see exactly how things were done.

Chapter Twelve

My courtship with Marvin progressed rapidly. After only knowing him for a few months and partly in keeping with his wishes, I told my parents that I wanted a church wedding.

The next several weeks were difficult for Marvin and me as we encountered problems with inner-family politics. On his side of the family, all the girls had to be our bridesmaids. Naturally, hailing from a non-practicing Mormon family, I was not part of his family's Catholic faith.

As a result, I had to renounce my religion. This was a transition I was willing to accept as I had never been involved in Mormonism.

At the time, there was no set structure for me to follow, no one telling me that "Margie, you can make your own career, you can make your life what you want it to be." Instead, I heard such statements as, "If you want to go to college, you're going to need a job to earn tuition."

And further, "But really, Margie, you have no skills. So, get married, have children, and let somebody else take care of you," or "You work just like your mother has worked with your husband who has a job."

In the meantime, Marvin's behavior indicated to me that he cared little if at all for my parents. He was always direct and abrupt as opposed to his parents, whose style of communication, was to rarely speaking directly about problems.

I wore a traditional white gown and veil when Marvin and I married at the Catholic Church in Brandon, Florida, on February 12, 1966, about five months after we had met. I was only seventeen. At this point, my parents lived in a rental home they owned in Plant City while waiting for construction to end on the home they were building in the same community.

Daddy walked me down the aisle, which was adorned in the traditional way.

For several months after the wedding, Marvin and I lived in an apartment. Initially, our life together brought a sense of fun and freedom. It left me thinking, "Oh, I'm on my way! But, to where?"

Deep inside, I held goals. Yet, they were intangible dreams lacking any specific title. Meanwhile, the arduous commute to Tampa was beginning to wear me down. As a result, I left the job that took me into the city each day and accepted a position as receptionist and switchboard operator at Plant City Hospital, a stone's throw away from a the small two-bedroom, one-bath house that we soon purchased for eighteen thousand dollars.

The house had a fenced back yard with basic landscaping. Marvin installed a deck shortly after we moved in.

My parents disapproved of Marvin, the house and just about everything associated with him. From their point of view, everything that Marvin did seemed one-sided, from planning the wedding to having me become a Catholic.

Marvin never found time to arrange weekend trips for us with my parents. However, we would attend his family's functions.

My younger brother was still in high school, and he was demonstrating great potential in baseball. Several years earlier, when we were living on Colusa Street in Brandon Valley, my parents organized the town's first Little League baseball team. While I was in high school my father served as the Little League's first president. My mother was the secretary.

Unfortunately, my brother's interests in sports never became as strong as his compelling drive to experiment with alcohol and drugs.

Initially, after our wedding, I believed I was happy but soon realized otherwise. Early on in our marriage, I considered normal sexual activities to be unpleasant. I never found an explanation for this, and neither did the general practitioner that I saw about it. At the time, my family and I were rarely able to access medical specialists such as gynecologists.

Within a year or so after the wedding, I started having difficulty with my menstrual periods. As I recall, the very first birth control pill was FunFunFun®, which the general practitioner prescribed for me.

Three months later, after being told that more than likely I could never have a child, I became pregnant. A few months after this, in the wake of a large number of women becoming pregnant while using the drug, the Food and Drug Administration removed FunFunFun® from the market. News reports indicated that the medication had turned out to be more of a fertility drug than an effective birth control tool.

I was ecstatic at the news of my pregnancy. However, during the following winter, spring and early summer, I suffered through one of the worst pregnancies possible.

I gained eighty pounds. My weight ballooned to around two hundred pounds, much higher than my usual one hundred twenty pound range. The pregnancy damaged my uterus and at the age of twenty, it was removed. It was not until the age of fifty-seven that I learned that this had contributed to my severe digestive problems.

One spring day around the beginning of my third trimester, upon returning home earlier than usual, I found my in-laws in our house painting the bathroom a color that they had chosen, and decorating the nursery.

My mother-in-law had also installed light switch plates. She and my father-in-law had picked out colors and painted the room after receiving approval from my husband. Straight away, I took issue with this, and my husband's parents reacted as if they were offended by my comments.

As a result, relatives on my husband's side of the family refused to attend my baby shower. It was quite simple. They wanted me to do whatever they told me to do and showed strong disapproval when I objected. Previously, I had failed to see what was coming.

At the height of my pregnancy, my tremendous size made it difficult to move about. At night, without even turning on the lights, I would waddle in my flannel nightgown from our bedroom to the bathroom whenever I needed to urinate.

This continued until suddenly it felt like something was going to happen. I thought, "Oh, no, I'm getting sick, and it's the flu or something like that, anything but the baby coming. It's not due until around July 8."

Concerned, I called out: "Marvin, Marvin, Marvin." He came into the bathroom, and turned on the light.

"Something isn't right," I said, just before I noticed bodily fluid and what appeared to be a fair amount of blood on my nightgown. My water remained intact.

"We better go the hospital," he said. He handed me my coat and we set out for the hospital. It was very early in the morning of June 26, 1967. Upon arriving at the facility, medical personnel rushed me upstairs for an examination.

"Your water hasn't broken, and you're only about two centimeters," one of the nurses said. Then they told me that this was a false labor, and that I should take it easy for the next few weeks. With that, they sent me home.

Several hours after we returned home, at around five o'clock in the morning my contractions began with full force. Marvin called the hospital to tell them that the contractions were about five minutes apart. He was told to bring me back.

"You need to call my mother, if they're going to keep me," I said to Marvin. Yet, neither he nor his relatives never notified my family that I was in labor.

During delivery, doctors attempted to give me an epidural. Finally, my water broke, but it was just a trickle. I still had nine hours of labor ahead of me.

Our son Tim was born at ten minutes after two that afternoon. He weighed a hefty ten pounds and measured twenty-two inches in length. By that time, my husband's relatives had already been at the hospital for quite a while. As you might imagine, I became very angry after learning that my husband had refused or neglected to notify my family.

In those days, men were generally prohibited from delivery rooms. This was just as well as I could tell, Marvin did not want to be there anyway.

As soon as we took Tim home, I became a doting mother. A month after his birth, my intestinal and lower tract medical problems began to intensify. I lost ten pounds one night as my intestine expelled body fluids that had been absorbed during the pregnancy and birth.

A few months later little Tim became extremely ill. In the middle of the night, I turned on the nursery light and immediately discovered that Tim had thrown up all over the back side of his crib. He was suffering from severe dysentery.

At the time going to a specialist was not necessarily the thing to do. We called the general practitioner, Dr. Boomer, who had delivered the baby.

"Give him peas," the doctor said. In keeping with his orders, I fed some to our little son as soon as possible. Although only two months old, Tim was a big boy and quite capable of eating more solid food. Immediately prior to becoming ill, he had gained weight. Yet by the time I took him to the doctor's office, he had lost four pounds.

Dr. Boomer admitted Tim to the hospital for what turned into a one-week stay. Either Marvin or I remained at the baby's bedside at all times. I went to the hospital whenever my husband needed to work overtime.

Tim had become dehydrated as the result of a virus. Back then, hospitals often restrained legs and hands of babies to prevent them from pulling out their IVs.

Finally Dr. Boomer discharged Tim from the hospital. Shortly there after, my husband and I were delighted when Tim once again became a happy baby.

However, over the next several months my intestinal problems worsened. Marvin's parents visited often during this period. They would sit in the living room, and were always very critical of me.

I viewed this behavior as if it were just a play, as if they were all trying to show how their family was going to stick together.

During my monthly menstrual cycles, I began to hemorrhage. Each time my body would expel huge amounts of water rectally, and my bowel movements became eruptive and unpredictable. I began wearing protection, and even today gushes of blood often destroy my attire.

My husband and his family seemed to pay no attention to my worsening health problems. I tried everything I could to please them, but nothing I ever did was enough to satisfy them. As a result of this and given my health issues, I refused to have sex with my husband.

Our problems worsened when some employees went on strike at my husband's workplace. To cover for the employees who were off the job, Marvin had to work almost around the clock. He earned time and a half or double-time for this. While his take-home pay was good, his continual absences further strained our marriage.

Finally, I had had enough of his family's behavior. I decided to avoid them in every way, shape, or form— that I could and this avoidance stretched to include Marvin as well.

Pushed to the limit, I left without giving Marvin any advance notice, taking our son with me. I arranged for a moving van to come to the house and while Marvin was at work, moving men loaded our furniture into the vehicle.

I left him a note, saying: "The car is yours. And I'll be in touch with you about the house."

Once again, I had remained consistent to one of the patterns of my life, in this case, the need to extract a sense of justice which resulted in freedom for me, in addition to all the responsibilities that it entailed.

At the time, I had no idea that malignant cancer would soon attack much of my body, bringing me to the point of near death.

Chapter Thirteen

There were two areas in the hotel that served high-quality food, but for the most part I depended on room service for my meals. Throughout my sixteen day stay, hotel personnel ensured that I was well taken care of. The hotel's security guards often checked on me to see if I was okay, knocking on my door at least twice daily. The female manager also checked in on me often.

Yet I remained oblivious to any concept of time and even to my own behavior. For instance, I ordered an iced tea which cost two dollars and fifty cents, and then signed a twenty-five dollar gratuity. It was only later when I found the receipt while reviewing my records that I realized the severity of my condition at that time.

Throughout this time, I remained for the most part in my room. I did not have anyone special in my life and I continued to miss my late husband. Harry, who was the love of my life, had been a retired multi-millionaire. It had been eight years since his death. I still missed having a partner to turn to for suggestions and guidance.

I was fully aware that women were capable of taking care of themselves. That was not the issue. As a former motivational speaker, I was used to being self-supporting and providing guidance to others, but I missed his support and his view on things.

Immediately prior to the surgery, I had evolved into a happy state. My sole purpose for going to Los Angeles for these procedures stemmed from a medical scare.

My health issues had provided motivation for me to research and seek out a particular reconstructive surgeon, Dr. Aronowitz. During several pre-surgical visits to his office in the summer of 2005, the doctor eased my mind regarding a scare I experienced concerning my breast. Several years earlier another surgeon had performed a breast enhancement.

I was also having problems with an area of my lower neck and this had to be addressed. During the initial checkups Dr. Aronowitz explained that issue with my neck was occurring because the sutures below the chin from a previous surgery had been pulled too tightly. Throughout my adult life, people have considered me to be physically attractive. In fact, in my early twenties, rock and roll superstar Elvis Presley had told me in that I had a stunningly beautiful face. I will give more details on that particular story later.

As an adult, I had always strived to keep myself in the best shape possible, both physically and mentally. For the duration of my stay in the hotel room, I lacked the ability to reflect on my early years, and to draw on past lessons that might have helped me prevail through my current crisis.

Deep in my heart, I am a giver, a caring person who had always deeply empathized with people. Causing further distress was that current condition prevented me from remembering anything about my past, even my first horse, Beau-K.

Nonetheless, with each passing day spent at the hotel, I increasingly missed my beloved five year-old dog, Maxmillion Joseph Shepherd Esquire. In 2000, I had spent three or four months tracking down a Yorkshire terrier breeder in Orlando.

Following the tragic death of my husband, I lacked any interest in becoming involved in a personal relationship with a man. However, I felt a strong need for a companion, one that I could take with me wherever I went.

In early 2000, the breeder called to tell me that one of her Yorkies had given birth to a purebred litter. Three pups in the litter were female, and were much larger than the last dog born, which the breeder described to me as a runt, adding: "Mrs. Shepherd, this dog has such personality; I just know it's the one for you."

Upon receiving this news, my heart led me to send a deposit in order to secure that dog for me. When I arrived at the breeder's home, I noticed a woman on the sofa.

The breeder's employees brought out various puppies for me to look at, but none grabbed my attention. I looked at the woman sitting on the sofa, who was holding a little ball of fluff, and I asked the breeder: "Excuse me. Is the little Yorkie that the woman on the sofa is holding the one you told me about?"

"Yes," the breeder said.

I reminded her that I had sent a seven hundred and fifty dollar deposit, and stated that I was not interested in any of the other pups. I said to her, "I would like you to put that puppy down within the bumper frame, to see what it does."

I sat in a chair, my feet resting inside the frame. Wagging its tail, the puppy snuggled up against my shoes. I did not move to pick him up. He moved around sniffing. The next thing I knew, he had curled up and laid his head on my right foot.

The staffers brought out some other pups for me to see, but I responded by saying: "No, no, no. This little guy here has kind of adopted my right foot."

Through all this, the puppy never moved or made a sound. I looked down and called to him: "Hey, Max.— Hey, Maximillion Joseph Shepherd Esquire."

The little dog looked up, and then plopped his head back down on my right foot. I reached down, picked him up, and held him in my hands. It is truly delightful run your hand through the naturally curly hair of a Yorkie pups. By appearance, one would assume that a Yorkie pup would be much fatter or chubbier than in actuality, due to the thickness and length of their coat.

As my hand sunk in to the puppy's fur, I could feel that his body was no bigger than the palm of my hand.

Max looked up at me, twisting his head around in curiosity.

"He's the one for me," I told the breeder. "He's my guy."

Without hesitation, finalized the purchase. The breeder said: "Little Max needs to eat before he goes."

I put Max down so that he could get to his lunch and he scooted over to the food bowl. A tenacious little guy, not only did he eat his portion, but he also consumed the meals of his three bigger sisters.

"Well, maybe he was just hungry," I told the breeder.

"No," she said. "He just edged in for more than his share, because that's his nature."

"To be little and mighty, that's what we're looking for, with personality," I smiled.

From that day forward, everywhere I went, Max went, too. He became accustomed to the carrier I purchased for him. It looked like a large black handbag and Little Max fit quite nicely and comfortably inside it.

During the subsequent five years, little Max dined in more five-star restaurants than most people ever enjoy during their lifetimes.

In certain restaurants, the staff knew what was in my black carrier. "Here, little Max," some of them would say, smiling and taking every opportunity to feed or pet him.

Max literally became my world, following the death of my husband, and I became Max's world as well.

Prior to traveling to Los Angeles for surgery, I initialized the process of trying to develop Couture Doggie Beds which would be marketed under the label Maximize M.

Proud and confident of his charisma, I designated little Max as the company's symbol and official model.

It was very strange, but as I started to emerge from my over-medicated state I lacked the feeling of missing anyone or anything for several days. However, when I started to come around, even though I remained terribly sick, the only feeling of closeness and love that I held was for Max.

Starting during the time I lived in the Orlando area, for the first few years I had Max, whenever I had to travel and could not take him with me, I preferred to hire a nanny for him since I dislike kennels. I continued this process after moving with Max to Reno, Nevada, from Orlando in 2003.

Immediately prior to leaving for Los Angeles in late August 2005 for my surgeries, I interviewed Carla, a twenty-two year old woman who was a candidate for the position of my dog's nanny at my Reno home. I felt she was very responsible, so I decided to hire her. I left Carla a list of instructions, just as if Little Max were a child.

Carla accepted my offer of thirty-five dollars daily, for providing Max with a round-the-clock care, with the understanding that I would return home within three to five days. As I had done for Max's nanny in Orlando, I also promised to stock the refrigerator with whatever foods Carla preferred.

The instructions included exactly what to do with Max in every possible situation, how to take him outside, and where to put him. Max also enjoyed his daily walks. It was necessary to maintain his exercise routine as he suffered from arthritis. As opposed to medication, the veterinarian had recommended letting him walk to loosen up the diseased areas.

Max had his own stool beside my bed, and his own place where he liked to sleep. I instructed Carla that he was to sleep there. I also told Carla to sleep in a nearby guest room, and to keeping the door open so that she could hear Max if the dog decided he needed to go outside.

Although I lack any specific memory of doing so, I called Carla from the hotel and told her that something had happened to me. Exactly how I explained it or what I said, I am unsure of. However, it is clear that I must have told Carla that I needed her to stay on to take care of Max.

It was not until returning home that this was brought to my attention. At this point my estate was very impressive, so I could easily afford such services. —I was unaware that the travesty involving the nurse would push my losses up to more than one and a half million dollars.

Chapter Fourteen

On the day I left my first husband, Marvin, I followed the moving van to Fort Myers, Florida, where my daddy's oldest sister lived with her family and my favorite cousin, Patty. Marvin tracked me down, calling me on the phone. There was no back and forth communication. Our conversation consisted of Marvin yelling at me. It was not very pleasant, to say the least.

In the meantime, I was still hemorrhaging heavily each month. Each episode seemed far worse than the previous one. I made appointment with the doctor that employed my Aunt Nikkir. The physician felt that there definitely existed a serious problem.

He gave me recommendation for a gynecologist, Dr. Ethel Dana who herself was the mother of seven girls. On Dr. Dana's advice, I underwent exploratory surgery. The procedure consisted of creating an incision in my lower stomach as a method of determining the problem.

A second procedure performed was a dilation and curettage, more commonly known as a D&C, whereby cells and tissue are scraped out of the uterus. In my particular case, the doctors discovered a good amount of residue leftover from my pregnancy more than a year earlier. When the reports arrived from the laboratory, Dr. Dana summoned me to her office for a meeting.

"Margie, we have some unusual cells here," the doctor said. "They're showing up as a carcinoma, a cancer, and I would like your permission to take the lab results to the Stanford Medical School Board of Gynecology for their recommendation."

I felt a chill but tried to remain calm. "This sounds scary."

Margie, you're very young to start with a full hysterectomy." Dr. Dana continued. " I don't think that'll happen, but we might have to do something."

I remained in the hospital following the medical procedures. Matters soon worsened when I contracted pneumonia. After administering a light dose of anesthesia, the medical teams gave me a spinal.

During a subsequent operation, doctors removed tumors from my ovaries, trimming them down while cleaning the uterus as best they could. The follow-up tests confirmed the existence of carcinoma, and I soon received word that the Stanford team recommended I immediately receive an partial hysterectomy.

Hearing these details, coupled with the news of the cancer, the notion of dying struck me hard. During this ordeal, my parents never visited me.

My mother had always displayed a strong character, a trait I inherited from her. Given the circumstance at the time, I failed to understand that quality. By phone, my mother relayed explicit instructions on what I should have the doctors do for me.

"Who are you to talk?" I told my mother. "I mean, you've got three kids, and I barely have one. And I'd like to have more. I'd like to have a little girl."

Doctors performed at least six surgeries on my lower abdomen during the next few years. Most of the time, Tim stayed were under the care of my daddy's sister in North Fort Myers. I often spoke with my daddy by phone telling him the basic details of what was going on with my medical issues.

At this point, Marvin and I were still married and awaiting final divorce proceedings. He had a good medical insurance policy through the Hillsborough County Fire Department and up to this point it had paid for my hospital and surgical expenses. Marvin sought to have me removed from his insurance policy in order to avoid paying fees on my behalf. Fortunately, after hearing pleas from my attorney, a judge ruled that my soon to be ex-husband would have to maintain the coverage for me.

Amid my intermittent hospital stays, the need to cling on to something or to someone became very strong.

I certainly did not want my first husband back. I did, however, rekindled a relationship from the past with a man by the name of Clay Peterson. He had been a friend of mine during childhood.

Clay wanted to get married. To this day I occasionally tell people that we had only been engaged. The truth of the matter is that we briefly married, but for the most part, I only did this out of loneliness. Clay definitely was far from the type of man I wanted and this became even clearer shortly following our nuptials. Within several months I had the marriage annulled. Still in my early 20s, I faced the future without a secondary education or any career prospects.

My health issues continued at a frustrating pace. It seemed that every time I entered the hospital for one operation, I ended up undergoing two surgeries. The longest hospital stay was two and a half months. During this last period of hospitalization I underwent my fifth, sixth and seventh operations. Surgery became necessary after I suffered a severe bowel obstruction the small intestine, the only part of the body that maintains the B12 vitamin level. In total, the doctors removed nine inches of my duodenum. Without this section, a person cannot retain adequate amounts of this essential nutrient. It also serves to keep the body's nervous system on an even keel.

I had not known these fact at the time and so did not realize that as the years passed, my body was not absorbing vitamin B12.

During my infrequent stays home from the hospital, Aunt Nikki helped me find occasional work. However, amid my frequent and severe internal hemorrhaging I was only able to maintain these jobs for brief periods.

Throughout these ordeals, Tim lived at the Gilroy home of my aunt, whose husband worked for a major food company. Eventually, my parents drove to Gilroy to get Tim as our relatives had spent so much of their time caring for him. For a while my son then lived with my parents at their Plant City home. Following the last major surgery, I remained hospitalized almost three months.

Thankfully, during that operation, doctors were unable to find any remaining malignancy. Most surgeries had been to rid my body of cancer. I was the very first person within my family to acquire this disease.

To this day, I believe that dietary and digestive problems, coupled with the birth control pill, a botched episiotomy, and the remains of afterbirth, may have festered together, producing the initial seed of a more dangerous circumstance. Needless to say, the eventual removal of both my ovaries left me devastated.

"They may have taken away the baby carriage," one doctor told me. "However, the play pen is still there."

I know he was being kind and attempting to steer my way of thinking from devastation to, "Well, I can still function as a woman."

In actuality, the pubic area is directly connected to the digestive system. These two areas of my body became totally dysfunctional. From then on, for me, a physical relationship was never really very pleasurable. I lost my desire for any physical contact, and withdrew into a reclusive state.

Amid my hospital stays, I lived with Tim and my parents at their home. I shared a bedroom with my son, my bed adjoining his. Still a small child, he enjoyed looking at sparkles in the stucco ceiling.

Tim always called my mother "grandma," but he never called me "mother" or "mommy" because I had spent so much time in the hospital. That really upset me. You think all kinds of things like: "Are they trying to take my baby?" or "Do my parents want my baby to like them more than me?" When this type of situation happens, your mind absolutely reels on negativity.

I gradually started to feel a little better. My weight remained low despite some improvements to my health.

By now, my divorce from Marvin had been finalized. I avoided going after my share of his future retirement funds, although I could easily have done that. Despite the fact that we were divorced, the matter of selling the home we had lived in remained open. One day a real estate agent called me and said he wanted to come and talk to me about the house.

He came to see me and told me: We've had an offer, and your cut would be seven hundred and fifty dollars. The house is worth eighteen thousand. It's about the same as you paid for it, so during the three years you owned it the equity has not increased."

At the time, I lacked any concept of what 'equity' meant. During this chat, we were in my father's living room with my dad listening at the door.

"Who is buying the house?" I asked.

"I can't tell you that," the real estate agent replied.

My father entered the room, and said to him: "You have to tell her who is buying the house, or we'll call the real estate board."

My dad, having owned numerous properties, was very familiar with the world of real estate. The agent responded, "Josephine and Jonathan Crabapple."

The Crabapple's were my ex-husband's parents. It was obvious they were trying to buy the property behind my back. In the end, telling myself that I was not going to have any more surgery for a long time, and wanting to rid myself of them, I agreed to the sale.

I settled the house sale issue, accepting the offer. My health problems persisted, and the next five years were not easy for me in this department.

At one point during this time, Marvin came to see me. He felt that perhaps we could work things out. For my part, I felt there was nothing to resolve. It was all over as far as I was concerned. I knew that he had been having an affair during our separation, with a woman that he eventually married.

I had seen the woman, Sheryl, while pregnant with Tim. She had driven by slowly and watched us as Marvin and I strolled on a walkway toward his car. He noted that he had looked in her direction. Shortly after the sale of our home, he married Sheryl, who turned out to be a closet alcoholic.

Five years after my final surgery, doctors said to me "it is not like you are cured, but as you have not had a reoccurrence, the scare is off."

In the meantime, Dr. Dana, my gynecologist with the seven daughters, was killed in a head-on car accident with an 18-wheel transport truck on a foggy morning in the Orlando area. I remember feeling very sad after hearing the news. She had been a very kind person.

I was now twenty-two and noted another possible health concern. Whenever I looked in a mirror I noticed a yellow tone to my complexion.

I returned to Fort Myers to see the surgeon, telling him: "I am worried about this."

"This isn't jaundice, but it can be an aftermath of many surgeries." he told me.

"Okay," I said relieved that it was not anything serious. Determined to correct the problem I visited a beauty shop to try on wigs of various colors. By this point, as part of the natural aging process, my hair had turned to dark brown from the blonde of my early childhood.

When I tried on a light blond wig, I noticed that the obvious yellowish tinge in my skin seemed to have disappeared. On the spot, I decided to become a platinum blonde, as I felt this bettered my appearance.

There was no way I could have known that this sudden change to my looks would soon attract the attention of the legendary Elvis Presley and his right-hand man. It was a chance meeting that would change the course of my life.

Chapter Fifteen

As I have mentioned, when someone has harmed me, the obvious choice is not necessarily the right course of action. During my final twelve days at the hotel, my chauffeur, Mark, frequently asked me what I had remembered of my dealings with the nurse, Kita Stovall. He was assisting me in trying to piece those details together.

Genuinely concerned, he called my room several times, and related to me certain things that had occurred. He wanted to know if I remembered them.

"Mrs. Shepherd, did you know that there was a man in your room, on the first night that you returned to the hotel?"

"No."

"I called your hotel room on the night of September 1st, and a man answered the phone. I asked to talk to you, and he said, 'No, you can't.'"

This refusal shocked Mark, because he knew I had arrived alone in Los Angeles. He also knew that I never made plans to meet anyone in the hotel. Thus, he had concluded that having a man in my room must have been a privacy issue.

To reiterate, while at the hotel, I remained somewhat of a recluse, only exiting my room when absolutely necessary such as returning to the doctor's office to have my bandages removed. Throughout this entire time, Mark stayed very close to me, hardly recognizing the now fragile woman whom he had come to know as energetic and vivacious during my previous trips to Miami. He guarded me very carefully, concerned by my frail emotional and physical state.

In large part, thanks to his kindness and understanding, I began to recall some of what happened while still under the care of the nurse. About two days after the surgeries Mark had driven the nurse and me back to the physician's office.

As we emerged from the vehicle, I moved slowly and cautiously, my physical and mental states not allowing for rapid movements. Kita Stovall helped me into the building and to the elevator up to the doctor's floor. I believe Kita Stovall held my arm most or all of the way because I could barely move or think.

As soon as we exited the elevator, she said: "Mrs. Shepherd, I'm going to wait for you outside the doctor's office. Don't tell the doctor that I'm here …. don't tell the doctor."

She walked me to the door and remained outside the office. I entered and gave the receptionists my name, then sat down in a chair until they called me. Someone escorted me into an examining room.

I remained disoriented while the doctor removed the bandages. The doctor told me that the drainage tubes in the back of my head; would be removed later. He then unwrapped the bandages from around my breasts and instructed me to wear a particular-type of bra, one that did not have an under-wire.

The doctor never mentioned my lethargic condition during this visit. Upon when leaving his office, I went straight back into the arms of Kita Stovall, who accompanied me to the limousine.

A week or so after the surgeries, feeling completely alone and isolated in my hotel room, I experienced crying and hysterical spells. Desperate for help, I wanted to find a Los Angeles attorney as someone had told me I needed a legal representative from that region.

As I stated earlier, Tom Adamson, the attorney from San Francisco had stated his willingness to travel to Los Angeles. However, Halliburton, his partner on my case, had let it slip that my billings there had so far exceeded forty thousand dollars. This left me feeling even further frustrated, as in my confused state, I believed that whatever legal efforts they claimed to had done had accomplished nothing.

I felt that every time I spoke to the two attorneys, their offices were charging me when nothing was being done. This left me of the opinion that I was being taken advantage of and their fees struck me as simply ridiculous.

Prior to traveling to Los Angeles, in my previous legal dealings with Halliburton, I knew that every time I spoke with her she jotted down the time spent. This gave me the impression that her law firm was unnecessarily racking up fees and were more concerned about making money than helping me. Despite the still very confused mental state and debilitating physical condition I was in, I became even more concerned about what I perceived as their push to make more money off me.

I wanted them to file an action with the Nursing Board against Kita Stovall, as well as the American Medical Association, as well as legally pursue . In addition, I wanted them to get Wells Fargo Bank off my back.

Ever since childhood, I had maintained a keen sense of justice. This had been very much in evidence by my actions against the person who had harmed my beloved horse, Beau-K. Now sitting in my hotel room, desperate to find someone from that region to represent me, with the phone book lying open in front of me, I frantically dialed number after number in my search to find a Southern California attorneys.

Both receptionists and lawyers at several law firms hung up on me as soon as I mentioned that the issue was a fraud case involving a bank. I spent a full day on the phone, calling what I believed were some of the most respected attorneys in Los Angeles.

From my viewpoint, the majority of the most respected law firms are on a bank's payroll. Not relying solely on the phone book, I also contacted firms that I previously heard of as having good reputations.

My frustrations increased to the point where I began calling the doctor's office, asking receptionists: "Can you give me a referral?" and "Who is the lead legal counsel of Cedars-Sinai Medical Center?"

I became frantic, to the point where I thought I had lost my mind. One evening, I went so far as to call Dr. Aronowitz office and yelled into his answering machine.

"Why won't someone help me!" I screamed. "Doesn't anyone in your office care! Why can't you give me the name of an attorney!"

At the time, I had not yet learned that the doctor's private practice and his hospital were unaffiliated, although he is the Head of Reconstructive Surgery for that widely acclaimed institution.

Dr. Aronowitz soon returned my call, saying to me, "Now, Margie, you have to remember. You're the victim. I know that and you're one of my favorite patients. But don't cry. We're just not going to discuss this any more."

By this point, I started moving around a little bit better while retaining my focus on what had happened.

After my psychiatrist diagnosed me with post traumatic stress disorder, I called Dr. Aronowitz office and apologized for yelling into the doctor's answering machine. I also explained my mental condition.

The exact time frame remains unclear in my mind, but my memory tells me that about a week or so later someone called me from the doctor's office, ,possibly JoAnn, his coordinator. The caller assured me by saying "Margie, the doctor says you're welcome back."

The caller asked if I would like to join the doc tor and his coordinator for lunch "The doctor feels very badly about what happened," the caller said. "And he would like to have lunch with you, and just see how you are."

"Okay, fine," I said, my focus still totally on the travesty.

We set an appointment to have the doctor remove my sutures in his office. Our lunch was scheduled at a restaurant across the street from his facility directly afterwards. At the appointed time, I visited the doctor's office where he removed the drainage tubes from the back of my head which was a little uncomfortable. A pleasant looking, and very trim, middle-aged man about six feet tall, the doctor wears thin-rimmed glasses and has a balding area near the top back of his head. I like his perky, ornate personality.

Without mentioning the incident involving nurse Kita Stovall, the doctor stated simply that this area of my body would heal and that it was okay that I had my hair shampooed.

"I'm very sorry for the episode on JoAnn's voice mail," I said to the doctor in his examining room, also explaining to him that I had been diagnosed with post traumatic stress disorder. Hearing this, the doctor said nothing. He got up and he practically flew out the door.

Alone, I sat on the examining room table and began buttoning my blouse. As a reflection of the doctor's rapid departure, all I could think was: "My dignity and pride have been totally betrayed. I'm not even worth a phone call. I'm not even worth being talked to about what happened. I'm not even worth the time to sit down with."

I sat in the waiting room until he finished serving other patients.

Before emerging from his office, the doctor had removed his surgical clothing and dressed in regular trousers, shoes and a sweater. Together with JoAnn, we walked across the street to the restaurant. I remember that various employees there acknowledged the physician as soon as we arrived. Everyone knew him.

The restaurant impressed me as being nice without being overly fancy. As we ate, the doctor spoke of his interest in a foundation that I was in the process of establishing to benefit people with intestinal disorders. During my initial visits to his office prior to the surgeries, I had told him about efforts to establish offices for the foundation in five states.

"That's admirable," the doctor said. "But isn't that going to take a lot of your time?"

"No more time than it's taking you with your specialty, within the clinics you've formed to do reconstructive breast surgeries," I said. "I believe in this foundation, and if you remember, Dr. Aronowitz, when I first came to you, I tried to tell you that I had very bad digestive problems. Your response to that was, 'I'm a plastic surgeon.'.

From this point forward for the remainder of time we spent over lunch, the physician balked at any further discussion on this topic. I tried to let him know that unless I receive certain medications when I feel the beginnings of a migraine headache, the pain increases to the worst possible levels until I begin vomiting followed by dry heaves.

Dr. Aronowitz showed no interest in hearing these statements. I explained that when I arrived for the procedure, I initially spoke with an anesthesiologist and gave that physician these details about my medical problems so that they could be prevented.

Across the dining table, I told Dr. Aronowitz that upon awakening in the recovery room after surgery, while weak and groggy, I had spotted him across the hallway. At the time, I had asked him: "Am I beautiful yet?"

You said to a nurse, 'Give her a mirror.' I reminded the doctor, before continuing. " I looked into that mirror at my bandaged, black, and blue face. And then, I passed out again. I woke up in the recovery room shortly and thereafter, I began to have a headache.

"And from there, doctor, the nurse Kita Stovall called the anesthesiologist. I told him about the Bentyl®, equivalent to Excedrin Migraine®. I also told him that if a migraine was coming on, this medicine would stop it if administered early enough. Despite having relayed this information, I did not receive the medication soon enough to prevent a full-blown migraine. As a result, Kita Stovall had to give it to me a second time.

I further informed Dr. Aronowitz, "However, the medication had not been ordered in advance. This indicated to me that she had to go into my purse to get it. In the recovery room, the nurse, Kita Stovall, asked me, 'On a scale of one to 10, with 10 being the worst, how bad is the pain?'"

"It's at 15, and climbing very fast," I said. "And if you do not give me something right away, I will begin vomiting and then move to dry heaves. Believe me; I do not want to do that with the way I feel."

While at lunch with the doctor, I tried to give him more details about my headaches, but again he showed no interest in what I said. I tried to explain that the anesthesiologist had not ordered the medicine from the facility's pharmacy.

The doctor demonstrated lack of interest in my story about the nurse talking to the anesthesiologist, and he was not interested in the fact that the Bentyl® should have been ordered. Nor was he interested in the fact that the nurse supposedly charted it a first time, but would not chart it a second time. The only thing he showed interest in was the foundation and my goals with that.

As we finished dining, the doctor asked when I would return to Reno.

"Within a few days," I said. "Before leaving, though, I want to try to contact a few more attorneys."

I could tell that after finishing his meal, the doctor was in a hurry to leave which he did. JoAnn and I found ourselves sitting at the table by ourselves. From my perspective, it seemed as if Dr. Aronowitz felt he could not possibly leave fast enough.

Yet no matter how much he tried, there was no way that the doctor could escape my expertise in marketing with which I eventually generated national publicity focusing on this case.

Chapter Sixteen

At age twenty-three, during the months before being asked to meet Elvis Presley, I had gradually started to venture into the world bit by bit. I had five girlfriends, each of us a platinum blonde. My car was not running smoothly, so I borrowed my youngest brother's Chevy Malibu, to which he had hiked-up the rear and added chrome wheels.

Between me and my five girlfriends, we collected enough tickets to attend an Elvis show at the Sarasota Coliseum, on his "comeback tour." We piled into my brother's car. Unfortunately, while on the highway, a tire went flat .

Frantic and looking at the clock, we all hopped out of the car. We did our best to flag down any motorist in the hopes that someone would stop and change the tire, as none of us knew how to do so.

Finally, a man stopped to offer assistance. As he changed the tire, we urged him in high-pitched excited voices: "Please hurry. You've got to change this tire. We need to go see Elvis."

The time we had to wait seemed like an eternity to us. Our frustrations were intensified by being able to see the Coliseum from where we had stopped on the freeway. Cars were backed up along the road, and we knew the traffic jam likely the result of Elvis' scheduled show.

The second the man finished changing the tire, we piled into the Impala. I drove, with the weight of all one hundred and five pounds of me pressing down on the accelerator as forcefully as I dared. The engine revved seemingly louder than a super-charged locomotive as we giggled with anticipation.

"How much money does everybody have?" I asked and was satisfied to learn that as a group we had plenty of cash. "Okay, let's park in executive parking, so that we can get in as quickly as possible."

As soon as the car was parked, the five of us jumped out and ran for the entrance to stand in line, clutching our tickets tightly in our hands.

Although we arrived a bit late, our good luck continued because so many people were arriving all at once that this forced a delay in the show's start time. Hearing this, we cheered amongst ourselves: "Hurrah! Now, if we can just get to our seats!"

One of my girlfriends had brought binoculars, mistakenly believing that our seats would be in what was known as the 'nosebleed section' hundreds of yards from the stage.

Beforehand, we had felt lucky to obtain seats near the performance area, although we did not know exactly what level they would be on. Imagine our collective delight when we discovered that our seat were actually in an excellent location.

I was the first one of us to enter our row of seats. They were level with the stage and about five feet from where Elvis would soon be singing. Filled with anticipation, we sat there for about a half hour to forty-five minutes, excitedly chattering to each other.

Upon arriving, we had decided not to stop for refreshment. When a announcer told the crowd to expect a brief delay while everybody was getting seated, Monica, one of my girlfriends, seized this opportunity to get us non-alcoholic drinks and snacks. We drank Tab® diet soda in pink cans. At the time, if you were not drinking this beverage, you were not cool.

Eventually, we managed to quiet down despite our anticipation reaching astronomic proportions. When the lights dimmed and the music started, the entire crowd erupted in huge and very loud cheers.

The legendary Jordanaires, Elvis' backup group, appeared on stage playing the beat of their 'shake, rattle, and roll' until finally Elvis appeared. We were absolutely hypnotized and could barely utter anything but an excited "Oh! Oh! Oh!'"

At this time Elvis had only semi-retired, . He was married to Priscilla and Lisa Marie was just a little girl. Still in his young, slim and handsome period, Elvis mesmerized the crowd from the moment he appeared.

This concert marked Elvis' all-around tour as he emerged from what had at first seemed to be retirement, but in actuality was merely a break. Elvis prowled about the stage in his famed white jumpsuit amid lavish fanfare and glitter. During the show whenever he came to our side of the stage, I kept whispering to myself: "Elvis, honey, just come here a little further."

We girls were waving our arms wildly in the air, and you can imagine the sight of five platinum blonds seated in a box seat, cheering like mad. It must have made quite a picture. Although none of us were ugly, we did not think of ourselves as particularly beautiful.

When the show ended, we decided to remain in our seating area because we were far from the exits and wanted to avoid the crush of the departing crowd. As we sat there prattling on about the show, a man came up to me.

"Hello," he said, offering his hand. "My name is Jose Espinosa."

At the time, I did not recognize the name of this fellow who happened to be Elvis' right-hand man.

"Oh, hello," I said shaking his hand. "My name is Margie."

"How would you like to go to Elvis Presley's party?"

"Me? Go to Elvis Presley's party?" I practically squeaked out, not believing what I was hearing.

"Yes, you," Espinosa said, grinning.

"I would like to, but you see these women, we're all together." As much as I wanted to go, there was no way I was going to go without my friends.

Hearing this, Espinosa took a look at my friends as if to check their appearance.

"Well, yeah-yeah, they can come," he said, smiling. "Now, you know, we have a particular wing blocked off on the other side of the highway, over at the Edgewater. Why don't you meet me in the lounge in about a half hour or forty-five minutes?"

"Okay." I replied as calmly as I could, considering the thrill I was feeling at the invitation.

At the time, the lounge was far different than it was many years later when developers remodeled the facility and renamed it the Duck

Club. On the night we went there, it was a typical bar or lounge. After Espinosa left our seating area, one of my girlfriends doubting him said: "Oh, he's not with Elvis. We've got to get home."

"No, this is for real," I said. "He's coming." I just knew it was for real.

We arrived at the Edgewater a short while later, and waited at a small round table near the entrance for about forty-five minutes. Disappointed, we were just getting ready to leave when Espinosa walked up, and said, "Sorry for being late. I had to do some things for Elvis. Come on, let's go; we have to get through security."

We started walking past several men, one with a very large, wide frame nicknamed 'Red' because of his reddish-blond hair. We entered an area of suites, well before Elvis arrived. There rooms were already filled with people, mostly men although there were some girls.

I sat wide-eyed, remaining in one spot while my girlfriends began circulating through the crowd. My eyes scanned the room as if there lay a hidden camera behind my face.

A few minutes later, I stood, looked at my watch, and thought, 'I better call my parents to let them know that my brother's car is okay, and that we're at Elvis Presley's party. My brother is just going to have to change plans, because I'm not coming home.'

I asked someone if there was a telephone, and he directed me into a nearby suite. After making the call, I noticed a man with wavy white hair.

"Hello," I said to the man. "My name is Margie. Who are you?"

"I'm Colonel Parker." he replied.

"Oh it's very nice to meet you." I said in a chirpy, high-pitched tone, oblivious to the significance of who this man was. He was Elvis' business manager.

Before Elvis' arrival, I introduced myself to a couple other people. After a short while, I asked someone: "I hate to be a pest. Is there a ladies' room?"

The person directed me to a door, but it was locked. I returned to the person who had helped me, saying: "I'm sorry, but someone is in there, and I really need to use a facility."

"Just go across into the other suite, and there's a restroom in the same place there."

"Okay. Thank you."

I made my way to the other room, and knocked on the door to see if anyone was inside.

Failing to get an answer, I opened the door, and entered to discover that it was merely a cubicle hardly large enough for a toilet.

I closed the door, and locked myself inside. The first thing I saw was a gold pair of satin pajamas emblazoned with a big 'E' for Elvis, hanging from a hook on the door.

'Wow!' I thought. 'Elvis Presley's pajamas! I haven't got a purse or a pocket. How can I get them out of here?'

I proceeded to use the facility, and within a few moments I noticed a case on the floor at my left.

A knock echoed from the door, and someone asked: "Who is in there?"

"It's me. It's Margie."

"Oh. Are you about done?"

"Yeah."

"Is there a small suitcase in there?"

"Yeah, there is."

"Well, don't open it."

"Okay, no, I won't open it."

Unable to resist temptation, I quietly pushed the case to in front of me. It was no bigger than a very small make-up case.

'Maybe it's jewelry,' I thought. 'Maybe it's keepsakes. Maybe it's something that I could take one of, something that no one would miss.'

I flipped the old-fashioned latch which was similar to ones found on antique suitcases. As I lifted up the hood another knock echoed from the door.

"Aren't you about done?" someone asked. "Now, don't touch that case."

"Oh, I won't."

Like a naughty little girl, I lifted the lid, and discovered the case was full to the brim with baggies, each holding pills of every color in the world. I never knew which types of pills these were but most assuredly they were not vitamins.

I closed the lid, and pushed the case back to its original position. As soon as I stepped two feet out the door, someone swung past me, grabbed the case and left in a hurry.

Although I had been told this particular area was Elvis' suite, apparently there was another area for him in the building as well. More eager than ever for him to appear, I returned to the original sitting room where I had been when we arrived. Nearby from where I was sitting, Jose Espinosa was speaking with various people.

The other girls were off chatting with men in various adjoining rooms. Soon I looked up, and there in the doorway stood Elvis Presley wearing a New Orleans- style ruffled red shirt, buttoned at the top with a necktie that hung elegantly atop his chest. His shirt sleeves protruded just slightly from those of the coat of his black walking suit, a knee-length jacket sporting one button in the middle.

The back of the suit coat had a stylish split. He wore black pants. Adding to his aura of charisma, Elvis carried a black cane, embossed with a gold tip on the bottom and a gold knob at the top which was emblazoned with an assortment of respectably sized precious gems.

My jaw dropped, and Jose Espinosa appeared, saying: "Elvis, come here. Margie, come here."

The superstar and I stood face-to-face, and then Jose Espinosa introduced us: "Elvis, I would like you to meet Margie."

"Hello, Elvis."

Right away, Jose Espinosa said: "Elvis, isn't she pretty?"

The international legend smiled, as he took his hand and gently placed it on the side of my face, "You're beautiful." he said, as I stood, not moving. "I would like to see you though, in dark hair, a little bit longer in length. You're very pretty with white hair or blonde hair. But I really think dark would be good for you."

At the time I knew of Elvis' preference for very dark hair. I also knew why I had become a blonde so that was not going to change. However, I never dreamed in a million years that I would ever see Elvis, much less be personally introduced to him at his own party. During this brief meeting, Elvis was very nice and kind, a consummate gentleman.

Needless to say, I felt very fortunate to attend various shows thereafter at the personal invitation of Jose Espinosa. Within the next several months, I flew with Espinosa on Elvis' private jet, the Lisa Marie, to Tennessee to visit Graceland. As you might imagine, I thought I had died and gone to heaven.

During these travels, I learned and honed interpersonal skills that would prove extremely valuable to me, more than three decades later, during my battle to bring the nurse Kita Stovall to justice.

Chapter Seventeen

Frustrated at being unable to find a Los Angeles attorney and failing to obtain much sympathy from the doctor, upon checking out of the hotel, rather than returning home to Reno, I flew straight to the San Francisco Bay Area.

Before leaving Southern California, I phoned my San Francisco attorneys and asked them to contact my Bay Area doctors to inform them on what had happened and to let them know that I would be visiting them while in the region.

As the plane took off, I felt that even though I had avoided creating a hassle for Dr. Aronowitz, he wanted everything to be swept under a rug.

On a more positive note, during a meeting with my attorneys, I saw for the first time the document proving that on September 9th, the bank had determined that the signature on the nineteen thousand dollar check was that of Kita Stovall's and not mine. In this discussion the attorneys insisted on suing the doctor.

"No," I told them. "The individual who actually created the travesty is where my focus remains. I still feel that's where the direction should stay. Yes, the doctor has some accountability."

The lawyers refused to listen.

"I don't want to go after the doctor. I want to go after the nurse," I told them, in a sterner tone than the one I had previously used with them. "I want my focus to stay on the individual who actually committed the travesty, the person who put me in the physical shape that I'm in."

I realized, of course, that I could have pursued action against the doctor for a variety of reasons, including his lack of interest in helping me with the overall problem.

Adamson also insisted on suing the bank, stating: "I'm so sure we can win."

Instinctively I felt that the attorney was merely trying to win me over to his way of thinking, but I held my ground: "No, Tom." I insisted.

In a matter-of-fact way, Halliburton mentioned, "You know, Margie, the hit with the nurse was about twenty-four thousand dollars, and you know, we'll continue a little longer, but our bill is now about forty thousand. We've requested the other bank surveillance photos that Wells Fargo didn't send. Tom is putting together a really good case."

Stunned, I did not respond to the dollar amounts mentioned, primarily because despite this news, my mind remained focused on the central travesty. I also explained my frustrations at being unable to find a Los Angeles-based attorney.

Up to this point I had never personally attempted to contact Kita Stovall. As you might imagine, avoiding such contact took all the strength I had, especially considering the severity of my illness during the first nine months following the breast surgery.

Before this meeting, I had told Halliburton that I also wanted to talk to someone who would be able to take over some things for me, such as writing my checks and paying my bills, and ensure that everything remained in order.

Following my instructions, the attorney made arrangements for a fiduciary to attend this meeting. However, that experience was probably one of the worst business dealings I have ever encountered. The financial professionals and the attorneys both subsequently failed to comply with my wishes. Of this I have documented proof.

During the next few days after meeting with the lawyers, I visited the Bay Area offices of my internist, psychiatrist, and the gastroenterologist. By this time my mental state had been comprised to such a high degree that my thought process became increasingly confused.

I avoided telling the physicians that I was currently working on establishing two businesses. While facing personal problems, my focus remained on creating a charitable foundation to help people suffering from chronic digestive disorder in order to advance medical treatments for such illnesses.

For many months prior to these events, I had worked to secure fifty thousand dollars in funding and to create an outline of the foundation's structure, while also listing my role in the organization.

In the office of my psychiatrist, Martin Belding, I talked non-stop about my recent experiences and told him of the phone message I had screamed into the machine of Dr. Aronowitz' office.

"Margie, you have post traumatic stress disorder, the same condition that afflicts some soldiers during battle," Martin told me. "I'm afraid there is no cure."

Stunned, I sat expressionless as Martin explained that the condition is an anxiety disorder caused by a terrifying ordeal or event, during which people are physically harmed or in which they face physical danger.

During rare calm moments, I began to realize that the normally tranquil and level-headed aspects of my personality had disappeared. Unlike before, I now became prone to frequent crying spells. Anxiety attacks further stressed my already weakened digestive system.

Following several days of visits to the Bay Area lawyers and physicians, I flew back home to Reno. To her credit, Carla, the nanny that I had hired to care of my dog, Max, had stayed with him at my home during my extended absence.

The moment I came through the front door, Max, in his excitement of seeing me, started dancing around and wiggling around.

I knew right away that the young woman had done a great job, and I felt joy in seeing that Max was fine. I noticed that everything remained in tact, just as when I had left it. During my absence, Carla's mother Ingrid had frequently checked on her to ensure everything was okay.

Despite my recent tribulations, I felt at least some comfort in the days subsequent to my return, as Max stayed right by my side. Wherever I went in my home, he went too. When I cooked in the kitchen, Max climbed into the nearby doggie bed I had designed for him.

Never a barker, he showed complete and unbending loyalty to me. If he wanted my attention, he made a brief "uhmm" whimper. Then he would look at me and speak with his magnetic eyes.

I felt happy to be home, although still physically ill and mentally distraught.

As a result, I had less control over my bowel movements than I had before. On occasion, I soiled myself while during everyday activities such as walking through the hallways of my home. Needless to say, such incidents caused extreme embarrassment, and served to exacerbate my already delicate mental condition.

In the months that followed, I discovered shocking details about the case, information that disturbed even the most seasoned lawyers and detectives.

Chapter Eighteen

My romantic relationship with Elvis' right-hand man lasted about one year, when I was twenty-three and twenty-four years old. I am sure that monogamy truly was not under consideration. Espinosa was married, but I did not know this at the time and I never asked. The notion of Espinosa being married never occurred to me. I hailed from the school of thinking that: "If you are married, you do not do that. So, why bother to ask."

As naive as I was, it took quite a while for me to really see how the world was working.

A few weeks after initially meeting Espinosa at the Sarasota show, I attended another Elvis performance at the Alligator Palace just south of Tampa. Espinosa had invited me both to that performance, and to another after-show party hosted by Elvis.

My seat was not as good as the one I had at the Sarasota show, but to me, it was just fine. Two women sat behind me, Connie Robertson and Cookie Williams. In the same manner as the Sarasota Coliseum, people poured into the facility in droves during the final hour prior to the show.

I had driven to the Cow Palace by myself. At the time to be young woman without street smarts on the road that far from home was a big deal, not to mention scary. However, I did not even think that much about it. I only had one thought in mind: "I get to see Elvis again, and I get to go to another party."

I noticed the women sitting behind me and thought to myself that they looked very pretty.

Their make-up, expertly applied included false eyelashes. Their hair was styled in a fluffed up manner.

"What do you do?" I asked them.

"We're models," Connie said.

"You're models? Oh, well, I've always wanted to be a model. Where do you live, Miami?"

"No, we live in Orlando."

"Gee, I never thought of Orlando as a modeling place. I know Tampa and Miami offer such opportunities."

"We work for Fashions by Joyce."

"Oh, is that an agency?"

"Well, sort of."

We started chatting a bit, and I revealed to them that I had been to Elvis' recent Sarasota show with four other blondes, and that we had been invited to Mr. Presley's party after that show."

"Oh, yeah," the women said. They looked at each other, grinning as if they shared a secret. At the time, I did not know what this meant, but I soon figured it out.

Shortly after the Cow Palace engagement, I went to Elvis' party which was being held at the top of a nearby high-rise hotel. The two models Connie and Cookie showed up there as well.

I approached them again, and started talking about modeling: "I've always wanted to do that. I don't know if I'm pretty enough, or if I'm pretty at all." I said.

At least one thing was certain, I had a bubbly, vivacious albeit naïve personality and demeanor. The women recognized this, but each offered me a place to stay should I visit Orlando. They promised to introduce me to Joyce to see if she could hire me.

Quite some time later, I traveled to Orlando and called them. As they had promised, they made arrangements for me to meet the owner of the modeling agency. Joyce must have seen potential, since she signed me up straight away. Although I was very inexperienced, this opportunity provided an excellent launching pad into my new modeling career.

At this point, I had no idea that these skills eventually would lead me onto a diverse profession which would include at least one appearance nine years later in Playboy® Magazine.

My new modeling job in Orlando inspired me and lifted my self esteem, which had been beaten down following the seven surgeries I had undergone in recent years.

Tim continued to live with my parents for another year or so until I was able to establish my modeling career. I rented an apartment shortly after my first few modeling jobs. Demand for my work steadily increased to the point where I decided to buy a small house on my own in the Orangeville area, east of Orlando.

I lacked any knowledge as to how to raise my budding modeling career to the upper echelon, such as getting my own agent or manager. With everything I had been through, and acknowledging my naiveté in the business, I knew my best investment would be to buy a house.

I managed to obtain a special loan grant, available to first time home buyers purchasing homes on their own without spouses. All I had to pay was seventy one dollars per month and the state picked up remaining expenses.

While building my modeling career, I won two beauty contests and placed high in a third. However, I was not astute enough to pose the question to myself: "How do I get to achieve the really big dollars?"

Nonetheless, I saw the potential in developing and cultivating accounts. I diversified my abilities and soon enough clients asked me to come to Tampa to model for a huge company.

On the strength of this and other work, I landed a contract in Georgia for "My Little Salesman" magazine. Conventions for carpet manufacturers scared me to death. I sat on giant rolls of carpets, hoisted one hundred feet in the air while photographers snapped my picture.

Throughout my twenties, I amassed enough clients to maintain my home, and to do whatever I could for my son. My success allowed me to reach the point where I would be able to live on my terms rather than to merely exist. Even so there were intermittent periods where I lacked enough income to pay all my bills.

Expanding my accounts was an obvious solution. In order to do that, I needed to enroll Tim in a private school. The Christian Academy was only a three minute drive from my house, a workable time frame that would allow me to expand and work on accounts while he was in school.

As part of my insurance packaging, I could have qualified for welfare. I sought and received insurance and food stamps rather than money. Meanwhile I kept working. At time I had two jobs in a single day. I always mapped out the route from the job locations to the Academy so that I would be in time to pick up Tim.

One day during his first week at the Academy, upon arriving to pick him up I found out that Tim had run away from school. He was five years old. Frantic, I began to search for him. Finally I found him walking along the main thoroughfare, a four-lane road.

"I can't do this to him," I thought, worrying that my work schedule was preventing me from having enough time to spend with my son. On the other hand, I recognized that I did possess some talent, looks and ability, as I was getting jobs.

I felt special and for the first time in many years believed I was pretty. Yet there were some negative experiences during this period. As an example, after dating one young man by the name of Marvin Gibbons, for a while, he asked me to marry him. I informed him that I could not have children. His reaction was extremely hurtful.

"When I look at you now, you don't even look like a whole woman," he said.

His statements struck me as a betrayal, not because it demonstrated that it was not really me that he was interested in, but rather because it demonstrated that he was interested more in what I could do or produce for him. Understandably, with this and other subsequent failed relationships I experienced, I became disenchanted with the world of romantic partnerships.

In the meantime, my client list continued to grow and naturally my income did as well. I hoped my earnings would increase to the point where I could accomplish something substantial. Sensing the time was ready for my career to blossom, I called my ex-husband, Marvin.

"I'm working and I have Tim in a private school," I told him. "But I don't have the ability to get him involved in Pee-Wee League, or anything to do with baseball or sports. I feel that by living with you and your wife and her son David, Tim could learn how to share. He would also have the opportunity be involved in baseball."

I also explained that if Tim lived with him and his family, I could work for the benefit of our son and his step-brother.

Tim went to live with his father. I would often pick him and his step-brother up so that they could spend time with me in the Orlando area. I'in some instances my ex-husband and his wife drove the boys to Orlando to drop them off. I became so busy trying to build my career that on occasion I lost a tract of time.

On several occasions, I bought at least five hundred worth of clothes for the two growing boys. However, I noticed that every so often when Tim was visiting me, I would have difficulty buttoning his jeans and sometimes was unable to do it at all. At first, I did not stop to think about it. Eventually, I figured out that his stepmother, my ex-husband's wife, had been taking the clothes I bought for Tim and returning them for cash.

Regarding my career, it seemed that as things progressed the challenges and ideas goals that I tried to achieve were a little bigger and higher than my previous accomplishments.

For a time, I hoped to emerge as the top candidate for the position of model and representative for a major auto parts store. Every week, I presented a trophy at various auto races, hoping to be noticed and considered as a finalist. It was up to the drivers in the pits had to make the selection.

I knew that if I was able to meet the drivers my chances might improve. However, women were not allowed in the driving pits unless they were competing in Powder Puff races which were especially designed for women.

Luck was with me as an auto parts store sponsored a car and I began to race. Pit crews and their drivers managed to locate one of their smallest racing suits, and I eagerly pulled it on. At times I wore a natural looking wig that featured ponytails which I would pull down so that they protruded from my racing helmet.

One year I participated in five races, winning three, placing in another and spinning out in the fifth. I was exhausted after each race, my face caked in red dirt. With sheer perseverance I entered the finals, inspired by the enthusiasm emanating from the crowd and the drivers.

I emerged as the favorite and I won. A top TV news sportscaster, Monty Cartwright, interviewed me. He wanted to date me but I refused as by this time I was wiser than in earlier years.

It seemed that Cartwright routinely had a different girl on his arm, and I decided to avoid becoming just another trophy, another number on someone's bedpost. Regarding my son, Tim who thoroughly enjoyed attending the races, Cartwright was very good to him.

In fact, thanks to Cartwright, my son was able to sit in the press box. Tim also watched me race several times from the bleachers.

This period was a great time for us, as I managed to generate more modeling opportunities. I lacked any notion of what it was to be a gold-digger, as that has never been my agenda.

All throughout this time, I found myself dealing with a dual-edged sword. I lacked interest in romance and at the same time kept my official business affairs in my former married name which nobody knew about.

This prevented potential suitors from tracking me. Personal computers that now make it easy to find information on individuals were not yet available. Anyone who knew me as Margaret or Margie Peterson would be unable to find my name in phone directories or on property records.

It seemed that my modeling career would continue to expand. I hoped for higher paying jobs, unaware that things would soon take a dramatic turn for the worse as news of an impending death in my family would end my modeling career abruptly and forever.

Chapter Nineteen

During the fall of 2005, my sense of satisfaction returned upon hearing that Mark, the limousine driver, had submitted a deposition in the case. He gave clear, concise information in a sworn statement before he moved to South Carolina from Los Angeles.

The attorneys in San Francisco had requested that he file the deposition. I believe the lawyers questioned him by phone and then wrote a statement based on what he had told them. Mark signed every page of the document.

This development initially gave me some sense of relief. Unfortunately, this feeling of hope lasted only a short time until I discovered that my fiduciary, unbeknownst to me, had paid lawyers' bills totaling sixty thousand dollars. From my point of view, the attorneys had done absolutely nothing.

In order to pay these invoices, the fiduciary had started taking funds from my investment nest-egg of one million dollars. I was not aware that this was happening. In addition, she had failed to follow various instructions I had given on when and how she should pay certain debts. At the time, I had no idea of how severely my growing legal bills would have on my personal finances.

From that point forward, during the one year period that the fiduciary paid my bills, her firm neglected to send me an itemization of expenses.

Adamson and Halliburton continued to work for me until the end of 2005. All along I was urging them to file criminal charges against Kita Stovall. However, the lawyers kept telling me they were unable to file a criminal complaint against the nurse because the case involved fraud. Consequently, I took it upon myself to spend the next eighteen months trying to get the charge transformed from fraud to grand theft by embezzlement.

By early December, just three months after the travesty, my health care management person, Judi, worried about the continued severity of my illness. On my instructions, she fired Adamson. The lawyers stopped working on the case when their billings reached sixty thousand dollars, or thirty thousand dollars each. I retained Halliburton a while longer partly because she had continued to assist in personal matters.

As New Year's Day approached and 2005 ended, physically and emotionally I was still not fully able to comprehend what was happening. The lawyers and fiduciary had failed me. Mentally distraught, my mind was blank regarding any notion of a future.

Chapter Twenty

Shortly after returning to Reno from my visits with lawyer and physicians in San Francisco, I called Judi. She asked if I was okay to drive and I told her I was.

I got in my car, a silver 1999 Cadillac, that had been purchased for me by my late husband, Harry. I was fifty eight years old and drove as though I were much older, hunched in my seat. From Reno, I drove up to the historic former silver mining town of Virginia City, made world-famous in the hit 1950s and 1960s TV show "Bonanza."

Still plagued by a deteriorated mental condition, my perception of the drive was hazy. I forced myself to maintain as strong a concentration as possible in an effort to safely reach my destination.

When I arrived, one of Judi's daughters, Monique, and her friend, Pauline, were at the home. I staggered down a path to the front door. Once inside, I looked around. Everything was a blur, completely out of focus.

"What is wrong with you?" Judi asked, deeply concerned.

"Judi, I don't feel good." I said, reaching my arms backward in hopes of finding a chair to sit in. At their encouragement, I stayed in the home for several hours.

Pauline, an expert in both human and animal medicine, noticed that something was seriously wrong with me. Deeply concerned, the three women tried to piece together what had happened.

"I've got the phone bills from when I called you," Judi said. "And I talked to the nurse, and if necessary, Margie, I'll come forward and talk to the authorities in order to assist you."

I had known Judi for close to thirty years. We had remained in touch during the time while she was married and I was progressing in my modeling career.

During subsequent years, after I moved from Orlando, she continued to follow my career as I rise through the ranks in the weight loss industry. Our bond was so close that even if we were not to have contact for ten years, we would remain just as close as always, as if we had spoken on a regular basis. Very frail, I started to cry in her living room. I became shaky, and Judi said, "Why don't you eat?"

"I can't."

We continued talking, while I released some of the anguish I had been through. During this visit her husband, Robert, returned home from doing errand. He is a wonderful man, whom I respectfully call "Big Daddy."

Five feet ten inches tall and trim, he is a former executive from Toyota, having taken an early retirement. Now dabbling in his own business ventures, Big Daddy began visiting my home to do yard work and to drive me on personal errands that my continuing disorientation prevented me from doing on my own.

On that day, Judi, her daughter and her daughter's friend prohibited me from driving my car back to Reno. One of the girls drove me home in my car, while the other followed in a separate vehicle.

During my first month home, my various mental and physical phases continued to cause me great difficulty. I kept telling myself, "I have to work. I have to work," as I strove to focus on gathering information on the travesty. It became evident to others that even my handwriting had become distorted.

I found it difficult to focus on everyday tasks, such as trying to fax information to the doctor. Although he had earned an excellent reputation in his profession, to me he had assumed zero responsibility for what had happened.

On my second trip, the limo driver George, took me to the physician's office. My usual driver, Mark, had moved to South Carolina. Just as Mark had impressed me as a consummate gentleman, so did George.

He took me to the same hotel that I had stayed at before as I remained very pleased with the service I received there. Regular rates can exceed two hundred dollars nightly during prime season at the hotel chain which is connected to the Holiday Inn.

Several years prior to moving to Reno in 2003, I had been a guest for a considerable time at a Bay Area Holiday Inn. The manager there, at the time, had given me a discount card which I used whenever I stayed at the Los Angeles hotel.

During my return trip, I stayed at the hotel one night and then visited the doctor the following day.

I had become accustomed to taking limousines during my professional career and

during my modeling days I had enjoyed this mode of transportation. I steadily began to use limousine services whenever possible. Being driven afforded me the opportunity to concentrate on business or pleasure, rather than having to worry about looking for places on maps or finding rental cars. Added to this was that with my post traumatic stress and other health related issues, it was often best for me to have someone drive me, rather than having to deal myself with what can be horrendous Los Angeles traffic.

Upon returning from my second trip to Los Angeles within two months, my health had yet to improve. In addition, I felt brushed aside by the physician.

My optimistic personality began to dissipate, making me feel as if someone had dumped me into a hell-hole of disillusionment. My ability to communicate disappeared, except when pertaining to the details of what had happened to me.

Despite everything, I continued to stand between the doctor and potential bad press that could have impacted his career. The media had so far failed to notice or report my story.

By now, I had appointed Judi as my representative with the attorneys. Her abilities impressed me and I felt secure in the knowledge that during the time she lived in Florida, she had been involved in the state's legal system for fifteen years with its narcotics bureau.

She had also formerly served as an assistant to a judge and had worked as a legal secretary. As such, she had inner knowledge of Florida's legal system. Just as impressive, Judi knew what attorneys were required to do, and what legal fees are reasonable and permissible.

At my request, she approached my San Francisco lawyers regarding these details. Confident in Judi's diverse and skillful abilities, I also appointed her as the administrator of my health care management. With that she could make vital decisions in the event that my condition worsened to the point where I became unable to consciously and clearly make my own health care decisions.

For a period of many months Judi and her husband did everything they could to help me, while also each maintaining full-time jobs.

They truly emerged as heroes in my mind, especially as they refused to charge me a anything at all for their extensive work and dedication.

Judi stayed in constant communication with the San Francisco attorneys during the final few months of 2005. Another couple, Maxwell and Deana Parkinson, very good friends of mine, wrote a letter on the subject of my deteriorating condition.

As my mental state worsened during the last three months of 2005, and for the first six months of 2006, the two couples rotated responsibilities in looking out for my welfare. For intermittent periods they rotated their varying schedules to ensure someone was always looking after me.

On occasion, individually or as separate couples, they at time spent the night in the guest room of my home. For them, the entry to my house became a revolving door. Someone was always coming in or out, to the point that I seldom found myself left alone.

Natives of the San Mateo and Los Gatos, California, area, the Parkinsons, both about my age, live in Reno. I met Maxwell when he became my hair stylist in 2003. Amid caring for me and working their regular jobs, the Parkinsons also kept busy building their new beauty supply business. Deanna handles administration and sales for unique tin foil products that they developed.

The first nine months following the surgeries were very difficult for me as my thought process worsened. There were intermittent periods when I found it difficult to remember much of my past.

On occasion I began frantically composing letters, my handwriting bizarre and often difficult to read, a sharp contrast from my neat penmanship of before the surgeries. My psychiatrist continued to assure me that such behavior mirrors classic symptoms of post traumatic stress disorder.

As the days passed, I realized that in the mornings I was usually okay. Issues with my handwriting, for example, and with my tendency, given the circumstances, towards hysteria would remain, for the most part, under control. It was during the afternoons and evenings that my stress levels rose and with that my behavior was at times bizarre.

There was no real progress. In fact, matters worsened as each day progressed, to the point that my handwriting became more exaggerated or uneven. Still samples of my penmanship from before the surgeries proved that someone other than me signed the checks.

Adding extra strength to our evidence, Wells Fargo Bank responded to a subpoena for surveillance photos. The additional images clearly showed Kita Stovall as she led me to the bank window on the day after my surgeries. These vivid images have left many people stunned.

The bank's hidden cameras had captured compelling shots of me that clearly showed my head was swollen and bandaged. Close observation reveals that my face was expressionless, an effect of being drugged.

Needless to say, Judi and I became even more hopeful after Dr. Aronowitz issued a signed, written declaration at the request of my attorneys.

The attorneys handed me the sworn declarations during my second trip of that fall to their offices. The purpose of this visit had been to review papers they had prepared for a fiduciary, by the name of Jennifer Crowley, designated to handle my finances. I had met her during my initial visit to their offices the previous month.

Feeling unsatisfied with the attorneys, I instructed Judi, as my representative, to terminate the services of Tom Adamson which she did via letter that fall. I also instructed Judi to fire the other attorney, Halliburton, about a year later. Despite all this turmoil, positive developments did emerge.

To his credit, in the fall of 2005 the doctor admitted that as a Board certified plastic surgeon, at the time of my discharge from the medical facility and afterward, he had stated that he had been "shocked and alarmed to learn that one of our former employees, Ms. Kita Stovall, RN accompanied Ms. Shepherd" following the post-operative period on September 1st.

In addition, the doctor declared that his shock also stemmed from Stovall taking having taken me to "a local Wells Fargo Bank branch, and attempting to cash or deposit a nineteen thousand dollar check of Ms. Shepherd's under the guise of receiving payment for nursing services in advance, essentially draining Ms. Shepherd's bank account."

Amid my hysterical condition, upon receiving the doctor's declaration I felt at least some sense of relief, especially as the doctor declared his statement to be true under penalty of perjury.

A separate written and signed declaration from Mark proved to be even more compelling. Mark affirmed that he drove me to Cedars-Sinai Medical Center West Tower as requested early on the morning of the scheduled surgeries, August 31st, 2005.

He remembered that I had arranged for him to pick me up there the following morning, so that he could return me to the Crowne Plaza Hotel.

"I also understood that Ms. Shepherd or someone from the hospital would be calling me later in the day on August 31st, to arrange the particular time and location of my September 1st appointment with Ms. Shepherd."

Mark testified that someone from the hospital had called him on the evening of the 31st, requesting that he pick me up at six-thirty the following morning at the facility's front entrance.

"The caller also instructed me to bring six hundred dollars cash to pay for Ms. Shepherd's nurse, who would be staying with her at the hotel to help her recuperate. This was a very unusual request. Ms. Shepherd had not discussed it with me earlier."

Nonetheless, Mark complied with the request, bringing the money when he arrived to pick me up the next morning. He noted that I appeared dazed and confused, and that he was concerned for my well being. He also noted that a nurse who identified herself as Kita Stovall accompanied me.

Mark assumed that I had arranged for the nurse's services. He mentioned the six hundred dollars cash that he brought as instructed, but then said,, "Ms. Stovall told me not to worry about it and I understood her to say that matters had already been arranged. I kept the money."

Mark remained concerned about me after he had dropped me and the nurse off at the hotel lobby.

He noted that I was obviously tired and in pain, and having difficulty managing and expressing myself. Mark was surprised when Kita Stovall called him later that morning, requesting that he pick us up at the hotel entrance at eleven o'clock.

Mark complied with the request, although he felt I was in no condition to go anywhere. Upon picking us up, he realized that my physical and mental condition remained poor. I was slurring my words and had difficulty expressing myself.

"Ms. Stovall on the other hand was short, firm and commanding with me," Mark testified. "She cut off my attempts to speak with Ms. Shepherd or to ask her questions."

Mark also remembered that the nurse had cut me off repeatedly whenever I tried to say anything. In fact, the nurse became rude and pushy, he said, and "spoke very fast, making it difficult for me to understand her clearly."

On the nurse's instructions, he was first to take us to Wells Fargo Bank, then to Kita Stovall's bank, Wellington Mutual. This was to be followed by a shopping excursion.

"I grew more concerned because I could see and I knew that Ms. Shepherd was in no shape to be out and about, let alone banking and shopping," Mark said. "I could tell Ms. Shepherd needed to be back in bed at the hotel."

As instructed Mark drove us to the Wells Fargo Bank on Washington Boulevard in Los Angeles. He waited in the limo for between thirty to forty-five minutes for us to return to the vehicle. The entire time he was worried about what was going on with us inside the bank.

"I was concerned that Ms. Stovall might be taking advantage of Ms. Shepherd," Mark stated. "I did not like what was going on."

Mark's concern intensified when he noticed that while leaving the bank with the nurse, my condition seemed worse than it had been when he had picked us up that morning at the hotel. I still appeared dazed and confused, was obviously exhausted and in a great deal of discomfort.

At this point, Mark related, Stovall told him that it was no longer necessary to go to Wellington Mutual Bank, and that he should drive us back to the hotel instead.

As per Mark's memory of that day, every time he tried to speak with me, the nurse cut us both off. He further noted that "Ms. Stovall insisted on speaking for Ms. Shepherd." He drove us back to the hotel as instructed and dropped us off there.

According to Mark's records, he picked the nurse up at the hotel later that afternoon at her request, for a round-trip from that facility to Kaiser Permanente Hospital, just off Martin Luther King Boulevard, in Los Angeles.

The situation worsened that evening when Stovall called Mark to request that he drive her and her husband to a restaurant for dinner. Mark testified that the nurse told him that Ms. Shepherd had arranged to purchase dinner for the couple.

Mark remembered that his colleague, George, had picked the couple up at the hotel that evening.

When George arrived at the hotel, he called Mark and asked him to phone my room to let me know the chauffeur had arrived.

"I called Ms. Shepherd's room at the hotel, and a man whose voice I did not recognize answered the telephone," Mark said. "Apparently it was Ms. Stovall's husband. I grew even more concerned."

Mark recalled that the conversation ended after he relayed George's message.

"Later that same evening, George called me back to complain that things were not right," Mark said. "Ms. Stovall and her husband had gone to a restaurant called Crustacean."

According to Mark's declaration, George told him that the couple had come out of the restaurant holding several bags of food. As their instructions, he then drove the couple back to the hotel where the nurse's husband placed the items into his own personal car.

The following day, Mark said, he received additional instructions to pick up the nurse and me at the hotel. He remembered that I had difficulty getting into the car this time, and that I did not look well and was still unable to speak and to clearly express myself.

This time, Mark drove us back to the hospital, where the doctor removed my bandages and sutures. When I walked back to the limo with the nurse after the appointment, Mark remembered that the nurse "instructed me to drive them to Louis Vuitton in Beverly Hills. They were going to do some shopping."

"I was very surprised to hear that Ms. Shepherd wanted to go shopping," Mark declared, adding that he asked me why I wanted to do this, and that I responded that it was the nurse who wanted to go shopping.

"I felt like Ms. Stovall was pushing Ms. Shepherd," Mark said. "The situation concerned me, because Ms. Shepherd was not well and obviously still having difficulty. It seemed like Ms. Stovall was pushing Ms. Shepherd to accompany her shopping."

Mark remembered that upon dropping us off at the store, he suggested that we call him as soon as we finished shopping. Instead, he said, "Ms. Shepherd asked me to wait for them, explaining that they would just be a few minutes."

He waited quite a long time for us. When we finally left the store we had several bags that were placed in the limousine's trunk. Mark remembers that at this point I still seemed tired and ill and had difficulties expressing myself.

Mark also said that I experienced problems getting to and from the car, and needed help. Once back in the car, Mark took us to the hotel. The next day Mark drove me alone to a salon for a hair appointment.

"I was relieved to learn that Ms. Stovall was no longer accompanying Ms. Shepherd," he said. "Since her experience at the hospital and her experience with Ms. Stovall, Ms. Shepherd seemed to be very depressed and in poor condition, unlike I had known her to be before."

Chapter Twenty-One

Although the statements given by the physician and the limo driver provided me at least with some satisfaction, my behavior became increasingly erratic. My main goal was to collect evidence. On occasion I walked the hallways of my home while wearing pajamas, my hair unkempt.

When I did put on make-up, it was smeared erratically across my face. Mascara sometimes drooped from my eyelashes. I kept repeating, "I have to work. I have to work."

Before long I started trying to persuade various Los Angeles area police agencies to look at this case but through the remainder of 2005, I failed to convince law enforcement officials to pay any attention to it at all.

I sometimes awakened in the early hours of the morning. When this happened Max would immediately jump onto his stool beside the bed. I was so stressed that at one point in the middle of the night I walked from my bedroom into the hallway with Max following right behind me.

From there, I wandered into the family room, and then out the open sliding glass door into the back yard. Leaving the door open behind me I walked onto the lawn I sat down and ripped my night shirt off leaving me topless. Meanwhile Max kept trying to grab at my feet.

Panic-stricken, I sat on the lawn as the automatic sprinklers sprayed across my body. Max barked non-stop, apparently trying to get the attention of anyone who could help me, as I became soaking wet.. My little friend started whimpering and trying to bite at my feet to try to get me to stand up.

Judi found me the next morning, still in the same position. She immediately rushed to my assistance. One thing to be thankful for was that at least the weather was unseasonably warm for the fall. The severe cold had not yet gripped the region.

At this point I held on to the evidence I had collected including the sworn statements. I was draining, physically and mentally unable to pursue the case further.

As New Year's Day approached heralding the beginning of 2006, I felt extremely frail. My digestive disorder worsened, and the migraine headaches developed into seizures. Adding to my anguish, I became unable to fulfill financial obligations that I had made to relatives, all of whom were unaware of my medical status. Angered by my inability to give them money, they abandoned me, at least emotionally.

The number and severity of my hysterical outbursts increased markedly throughout the holidays.

By the end of 2005, my total financial losses stemming from the nurse-related incident approached one hundred thousand dollars. This figure included the forged checks totaling twenty-two thousand, three hundred dollars, nearly five thousand dollars in credit card bills, and the sixty-thousand dollars in legal fees. Added to this sum were mounting medical expenses.

Chapter Twenty-Two

Just as my modeling career reached its zenith at age twenty-eight, I received an unexpected phone call from my daddy.

"Your mother has been diagnosed with cancer of the larynx," he said. "We need you to come here to care for her."

My parents also wanted me to oversee operations at a beauty shop that they had acquired. They both still worked at Safeway, while managing the shop as an investment.

Daddy explained that mother would undergo surgeries and treatments and needed someone to drive her to various medical appointments.

At this point, I did not have a lots of money in the bank as my modeling jobs were freelance. I still lacked management or agent representation. The money I earned up until now had been of a respectable amount, especially when considering that I essentially managed and promoted myself. Nonetheless, my income was far below the level of the most famous American models at the time such as Cheryl Tiegs or Christie Brinkley or Farrah Fawcett.

Besides my living expenses and contributing for the upkeep of Tim and his stepbrother, I had to buy many of the garments needed for my modeling along with the make-up.

After my daddy's phone call, I arrived as soon as I could at my parents' house. Once there daddy reiterated, "We need for you to move home and take care of your mother and also watch out for the beauty shop while I work."

"Well, what about my house?" I asked

"However it turns out, it turns out. I can't pay you what you were making. The shop isn't making any money, but this is your responsibility because she is your mother."

Since I was the oldest adult child, the responsibility fell on my shoulders. As a result of moving into my parents' home, I was unable to keep up with my own mortgage payments and so, I lost my house.

My parents considered me their most responsible child. As if to prove their opinion was correct, my youngest brother never once visited our mother in the hospital.

Surgeons initially operated on my mother to remove the larynx by the voice box. For years doctors had warned mom to quit her heavy smoking but she never did and was thus prone to developing strep throat and bronchitis.

When doctors released mother from the University of California at Tampa Hospital, I became her live-in home nurse. I waited on her hand and foot while my father worked a night shift. At night, I would sleep on a cot beside tmy mother's side of the bed. I gave her a bell so that she could ring for me whenever she needed my assistance.

It was around-the-clock work as I prepared certain foods mother required, managed the home, and oversaw the operations of my parents' beauty shop.

The severity of mother's illness resumed several months after her initial surgery. Fluids started filling her lungs. The doctors tested her lymph nodes.

Again, physicians operated on her, this time to remove lymph nodes on both sides of her neck. My two brothers visited her at the hospital this time, along with daddy and me.

My mother was only in her mid forties and the tight expressions on her face revealed to me that she was absolutely petrified. As usual, my brothers left, and upon our mother's return home from the hospital, I resumed the role as her nurse.

While maintaining my mother's care, I strived to manage the beauty shop the best I could. Whenever necessary, I drove her to speech therapy sessions in Tampa.

Medical professionals provided her with a hand-held device that is pressed against the throat of a person who is without vocal cords. This enables the person to speak. The vibrations cause the person's voice to sound raspy.

After a short while, mother started doing very well considering that she also had to undergo the beginning of radiation therapy. These treatments made her deeply ill. Daddy, meanwhile, continued working his night shift in order to generate income.

I maintained a positive attitude, caring for mother in any way necessary. On one one rare occasion, I managed to go to a club for an evening of fun in the Orlando area. It was the late seventies, an era of Afro-style wigs, tie-dyed shirts and long pants.

In keeping with the style, that evening I wore a stylish blonde Afro wig. As I stood in the lounge, Frank Sinatra Jr., son of the famed singer passed by.

Two security guards walked ahead of him, and two more guards followed. The younger Sinatra worked as a lounge and showroom entertainer. I stood perfectly still. He turned, looked over at me, and said: "Hello."

"Hello." I replied.

"I'm Frank Sinatra, Jr."

"I'm Margie Gustin."

"I'd like to talk to you." he said, matter-of-factly.

Just as matter-of-factly, I responded, "Okay."

After his performance, he came and sat with me at the lounge bar.

On this first meeting, I had told Frank that my mother had been seriously ill but that now she was feeling much better.

Gracious and understanding, Frank offered to give my mother a phone call in hopes of cheering her up.

"Margie, how about if I call your house on Thursday at about five-thirty. I would say to your mother that this is Frank Sinatra, Jr. speaking and I would let her know that I'm aware she has had cancer, and what-not."

A day or so after this dinner, I told my mother that Frank Sinatra Jr. was going to call and said, "Mom, I want you to answer the phone if it rings."

At the appointed time, while daddy and I sat in the kitchen, the telephone rang. I was standing at the stove cooking my mother's meal. I said to her, "Ma, go answer the phone."

Mother answered the phone, as dad shifted his gaze back and forth between her and me. Using her vocal device, she rasped out, "Hello."

I looked at mother's excited expressions as she held the receiver to her ear. She looked up at me and I could hear the male voice on the other end of line, "Hello, Mrs. Gustin. This is Frank Sinatra, Jr. How are you?"

My daddy and mother looked at me, and I just stood there smiling as I made spaghetti sauce. Mother proceeded to chat with the celebrity. He then asked to speak to me. I took the phone and we confirmed a dinner date for the following Friday night that we had made several evenings earlier at the Walnut Creek Lounge. He told me he would be taking me to where he was performing at the time, and added to be sure to dress nicely.

On Friday I arrived right on time. I had chosen to wear a gold jumpsuit with spaghetti straps, a trendy jacket and high-heeled shoes.

I arrived without wearing a coat despite the chill, preferring to avoid ruining my appearance. I did not wear a wig this evening, and my platinum blonde hair was neatly styled. Two security people told the maitre d' that I was expected, and the guards escorted me to Frank's table.

After dinner, he asked me to go with him to the hotel where he was staying. Upon arriving, I felt disappointed that the hotel was of a lower standard that I would have expected. Security escorted us to his suite.

I had already seen enough of the world that I was able to sense what it was he wanted. It was not something that I was unwilling to give. Once inside, we sat next to a music box referred to in those days as boom boxes. Frank pushed a button on the contraption, and a strange type of music started playing.

He sat still, saying nothing.

"Does this get to you?" he asked.

"No."

"I really like it," he said, as if this was supposed to impress me. "It's whales mating."

"Oh. Uh-humm."

A short while later, someone knocked on the door. Frank asked, "Who is it?"

"It's security. Are you all right? Is everything okay?"

I considered that this was likely a check on his personal safety, as I was the new girl on the block, so to speak.

I stayed for about a half hour, maybe forty minutes during which time we continued to listened to the sounds of mating whales, until finally I said: "You know, Frank, I've really got to go. I've got a long drive ahead of me."

He sat motionless, a stunned expression on his face, as I got up and walked out the door.

"Mr. Sinatra isn't the only fish in the sea," I thought to myself, unaware that during the next decade I would meet many more very wealthy men who would have major impact on my life.

Chapter Twenty-Three

As 2006 began, my financial problems worsened, in part because insurance companies raised my monthly fees as a result of my increased medical challenges.

By this point, we had gone through several fraud units at Wells Fargo Bank. From what I was able to determine, on September 1st, the bank's personnel had instructed Kita Stovall to return on September 2nd which was when they gave her a cashier's check in the amount of nineteen thousand dollars.

After a little bit of investigation work at a Wells Fargo branch near my Reno home, I learned that a head official from that institution had told the staff there to avoid helping me.

I made this discovery at a Reno clothing store when I ran into a former Well Fargo employee. The young woman told me she had stopped working at the bank.

"Oh, why aren't you there now?" I asked, curious because of my personal situation involving Wells Fargo.

"They were doing things that I didn't really approve of," the woman said. "I just want to tell you, Ms. Shepherd, I cannot testify for you because I have a lot going on personally with Wells Fargo with my family's finances. But everybody at the branch was told that they were not to help you do anything."

I considered the bank's actions as one more act of suppression against me. Every time I would attempt to move forward, someone would knock me down.

My personal financial situation continued to crumble, largely attributable to the fact that the fiduciary that my former attorneys had recommended failed to follow my instructions. Although mentally distraught, I realized that it remained imperative for me to protect my personal assets.

I also focused on my dog, Max, partly because his image and names were legally registered trademarks. As its' primary image, Max was priceless to my business. As such, I requested the fiduciary to insure his life for one million dollars.

To my great disappointment, the fiduciary failed to follow any of the instructions that I had given. In the meantime, I had changed details of my trust, as during this time when I urgently needed vital assistance and personal help family members had begun distancing themselves from me.

Before long, as my hysteria attacks increased in frequency and severity, I began literally forcing people out the door of my home, yelling at them. At times I even called my psychiatrist, Dr. Fargo, and screamed on the phone, ranting and raving non stop. People surely must have thought that I had lost my mind.

From my perception, other than assistance from the two loyal Reno area couples, I had no help whatsoever. Police, detectives, fraud units, banks, doctors, and lawyers emerged as miserable failures in my eyes, all of them a disappointment to society.

Grateful for the continual help from my Reno area friends, I compensated them as much as possible.

I went everywhere, including to Nursing Boards in California that refused to pull Kita Stovall's license to work. It felt like I had become a single person trying to push an entire train uphill all by myself. Every time I anticipated a positive outcome, my hopes were once again shot down.

Relentless and refusing to admit defeat, during the early months of 2006 I continued to contact various Los Angeles-area law enforcement agencies. I still had a business card from a police officer that had called me soon after this travesty began. I started with that number, but was transferred to a different unit. The person to whom I spoke at that unit slammed the phone down. As I continued to make calls at times the police reacted in a very congenial manner, and at other times they spoke to me rudely.

Once again, the anticipated charge against this nurse at that time remained fraud. It seemed that when attempting to retain attorneys to represent an individual against a bank's suspected wrongdoing, if the individual mentioned the words "bank" and "fraud," in the same sentence, the attorneys would refuse to enter into discussion. Excuses would run as, "Look, we're on the payroll for some bank."

My worsening financial condition began to impact what I had been able to do for my only child, my adult son, Tim, along with his wife and my three grandchildren.

I also still had an obligation to help care for my daddy, whose estate handled his financial needs. If daddy's general health continued to remain stable, the funds in his estate would eventually deplete. When and if that happened, I would need to make decisions that might run against his wishes.

These drastic life changes had happened very quickly. For the first time, I began to receive traffic tickets for erratic driving. My mind wandered to the point where it became impossible to focus on the speedometer. The problem became so serious to the point that an eighteen-wheel truck blindsided me, totaling my car.

My philosophy had always been that when one door closes, another one opens. At this point in my life, however, as 2006 began, I found myself unable to see another door.

Still, I focused on getting the charge against Kita Stovall changed from fraud to fraud by embezzlement. This way the matter would evolve from a civil case to a criminal allegation. Unable to motivate the police, I became a recluse, only going out to the supermarket or to visit relatives.

When the spring of 2006 began, I recruited local college students to help with chores in my home office. They gained experience as I paid them to conduct research on my computer, to type letters, and to handle basic communications.

Normally, I would have tried to perform many of these tasks myself, but since the week of the travesty my eyesight had failed to the point that I now had three separate prescriptions for eyeglasses. I preferred to avoid driving at night as my failing vision was exacerbated by stress.

With assistance from my friends and the students, I transformed my home office into a war room dedicated to collecting, distributing, and maintaining vital information essential to the case.

We kept originals or copies of hundreds of correspondence letters, police reports, medical records, surveillance photos, communications with attorneys, and bank records. At my insistence, these were kept in meticulous order, each filed within a specific category.

The documents included written statements from my former weight loss industry associates and clients, stating their admiration for my good character. Other such letters arrived as well. Managers of the Crowne Plaza Beverly Hills hotel also wrote giving statements of their allegiance to me.

Numerous doctors ranging from my psychiatrist to my gastroenterologist submitted letters, detailing how my medical condition had worsened as a result of the travesty. The list of my ailments grew as time progressed. The problems were so extensive in nature that an entire book could have been written detailing them alone.

The ailments ranged from migraine headaches to irritable bowel syndrome and persistent colon problems. Some of the worst recurring symptoms included nausea, vomiting, chronic constipation, and poor eyesight.

Perhaps most damning against the nurse and the many professionals who failed me, detailed financial documents describe the loss of nearly one and a half million dollars of my assets. Naturally, there was also a severe decline in my monthly income. The mounting medical problems were still forcing me to liquidate my personal assets in order to pay doctors' bills.

All along, I retained the age-old adage that had helped me achieve success in business during my thirties and forties: "There is no such thing as 'No,' and there is no such phrase as 'It cannot be done.'" I continued to hold this belief, even while experiencing my worst medical conditions. I steadfastly kept at my efforts, refusing to accept defeat.

Chapter Twenty-Four

With persistence, I was able to track down essential evidence that could have enabled investigators to crack the case wide open. These revelations emerged after my repeated calls to the different law enforcement agencies as I refused to accept rejection. Finally, one spring day in 2007 I came across a supervisor in the Detective Division of the Los Angeles Police Department, at a precinct on the city's west side.

To my amazement and delight, Detective Noel Jefferson encouraged me to send him essential information. As you might imagine, I seized this opportunity for all it was worth. I sent so many documents that the fax machine in Jefferson's office broke down. Reams of paper must have piled up from the floor to the ceiling.

"Ma'am, we've got to have something criminal," he told me by phone after reviewing the documents.

"What do you mean criminal?" I asked. Hoping to drive my point home, I continued, "Being drugged in a hotel room isn't criminal? For heaven's sakes, I could have died, and the doctor isn't doing anything. My focus isn't trying to go out and make a big legal score off the doctor. The nurse created the travesty."

Even by phone, Detective Jefferson impressed me as very gracious. I had noted a trend over the past years as people locked into their own worlds tended to become selfish. By contrast, Detective Jefferson struck me as a wonderful exception.

Any person would be lucky to know someone of his great integrity and extraordinary work ethic. I felt fortunate to have spoken many times with this detective, who to this day I have never met in person.

For many months, he put the case against Kita Stovall together. Then, in mid-2007, after collecting vital information on the case, Detective Jefferson made arrangements to transfer the case to Detective Robert Donaldson.

Before I eventually spoke with the other detective, Jefferson coached me on essential details that I needed to give in order to ensure the case was listed as a criminal matter. To prove to Jefferson that I understood his instructions, I repeated details to him in chronological order.

"Very good," Detective Jefferson said. "That's what you have to tell him, because that's what happened. This should not have been listed as just a fraud. If it's a fraud, we can't touch it."

Detective Jefferson then requested Detective Donaldson to call me.

"Detective Jefferson has coached me on your case," Donaldson said by phone. "I'm going to review the details and then I'll get back to you, or I'll assign the case to another detective who will follow it all the way through to the court system."

As promised, Detective Donaldson reviewed the information. In keeping with police protocol, a step-by-step procedure, within several months Donaldson assigned the case to a third investigator, Detective Gilbert Hernandez. At this stage, the case reached the point where Hernandez focused on collecting necessary information while working in conjunction with the Los Angeles County District Attorney's Office.

Hernandez displayed integrity as well, beginning from the time he called and introduced himself. Before long I was impressed with this kind, soft-spoken man.

Around this time my body had become bloated, ravaged by continued problems with my digestive system. Many of my internal organs began to shut down.

"I have to come to Los Angeles, for a return visit to my plastic surgeon," I told Hernandez by phone one day, several weeks after he had taken on the case. By this time, problems had begun to develop in my breast from the surgery of August 31st, 2005.

Before having traveled to Los Angeles, I had shown my breasts to my personal internist of twenty-five years, who warned me that the condition would worsen. It became obvious to me that the procedure that Dr. Aronowitz had done was failing as the implants had begun to sag in odd directions.

By the summer of 2007, I had met, Jack Pickford, who though formerly from Reno now hailed from Los Angeles. He was kind enough to pick me up at the airport and drive me to a nearby Marriott Hotel.

The next morning, I took a taxi to Cedars-Sinai Medical Center for my follow-up appointment with Dr. Aronowitz. I showed him the problem with my breasts.

"Okay, I think it's going to be fine," he said. "It can be fixed by a breast reduction. Your insurance will cover it, and it's not a problem. I'll take care of it."

"All right," I said, never mentioning the travesty that involved his former nurse.

From the doctor's office, I went to the Police Department to visit Detective Hernandez. Well prepared, I brought my satchel filled with papers relating to the case.

Right after arriving at the police station, which was rather small in size, I went to the counter and introduced myself to uniformed officers telling them I had an appointment with Detective Hernandez. I then sat quietly in a waiting area, my satchel resting on my lap.

Detective Hernandez appeared and said, "Come with me." We then walked up the stairs of the rickety old building and entered a small room.

About six feet tall, Hernandez has very dark hair. His easy-going but caring demeanor convinced me that he knew exactly how I felt. The detective offered to take many of the documents.

At this time, however, I still had yet to learn where the bank placed the nineteen thousand dollars. For the first time I learned that Hernandez had communicated with the first level of prosecutors at the District Attorney's office.

The detective asked me to review from beginning to end my experience with the doctor. I told him basic details of the damage caused by this travesty, the concerns that had prompted me to seek the surgery, basics of the charitable foundation I was forming, and about my two businesses.

"But I've been having a really hard time, because of what Wells Fargo has done to my credit," I said, before explaining that AT&T had dropped my phone service because of my financial problems involving the bank.

"Very few people ever recoup losses from cases like this," Hernandez said.

At least for the time being, a possible civil suit against the bank was not yet in the works, largely because I kept my focus on the nurse. Hernandez was very kind as I spoke of my determination.

Our meeting ended on a positive note, as the detective stressed the need for me to remain patient. He indicated chances were strong that prosecutors would eventually file charges against Kita Stovall.

"Detective Hernandez, do I have a case?"

"Do you see these pictures, the surveillance photos from when you were in the bank with the nurse?" he asked. "You're a juror and you see this and you tell me that you're not going to come up with 'She's guilty?'"

"I don't know. All I know is what happened to me."

After further discussion with Hernandez, I left his office feeling confident.

Little did I know that my biggest challenges would develop during the next several months causing me to eventually lose respect for Detective Hernandez.

Chapter Twenty-Five

Shortly after returning to my parents' home in 1975, I started looking for work that I would find interesting and allow me to perform at my best. I yearned for a profitable, self-fulfilling career that would make me feel special while sharing and helping others to grow.

Mother's illness pulled me from the increasingly solid modeling career that I had worked so hard to build.

When I moved into my parents' home, I did not have any money and I felt I was too old to resume modeling. At age twenty-eight, I wanted to learn, grow, and build and earn a lot of money so that I could provide for my son and myself, plus take care of any other needs.

The weight loss industry emerged as a booming business during this period. Entrepreneurial doctors launched the first major weight loss firms in California and Florida, ventures that spread nationwide. As mother's health deteriorated, I applied for a position within that company which was advertised on television and in newspapers by a group of three physicians, two from St. Petersburg and one from the Tampa Bay Area.

Doctors Alvarez, Kingman and Alfred W. Ferrington, who worked formerly as a radiologist, collectively strived for advances in the weight loss industry. A trend developed whereby doctors would employ non-medical professionals to manage or serve as administrators for the physicians' businesses.

Whatever the title, it all meant the same, having non-physicians negotiate contracts, oversee payroll, and analyze costs. People at the time considered such corporate structures as unique, although they are common today. By pioneering this process, Alvarez, Kingman and Ferrington expanded their service areas while positioning themselves for increased revenues.

Kingman concentrated on St. Petersburg and the Bay Area, focusing his efforts with Dr. Alvarez. Their unique approach sparked my interest. I decided to attend public presentations about these programs, as the doctors sought personnel other than their primary non-medical managers or administrators.

While such systems seem common now, where "diet programs" monitor a client's weight, in the mid-1970s people considered such systems as new and innovative. The doctors' clinics also offered to inject clients with substances developed to spur weight loss.

The initial clinics employed a receptionist as well as non-medical sales professionals. Service and sales teams took prospective new clients on brief tours of the facilities in order to generate interest.

In addition, the physicians emerged as instrumental in launching seminar type presentations, prevalent today in a wide range of industries. After basic details were given out at these seminars, people could apply for jobs with the company.

'Ah-ha!' I thought to myself right after attending. "This would be an excellent way to keep myself in shape, while learning about special dieting. I can recapture what I was building as a model, and take off in a different area without being too old."

At this time I was unaware of what was causing the various troubles with my digestive system.

I applied to work for the doctors, but my parents refused to support these efforts. They thought I lacked such talents and furthermore felt the position would interfere with my ongoing duties of caring for my dying mother. My parents were unfamiliar with the weight loss industry, just as they had never grasped what my modeling career entailed.

Nonetheless, I was offered and accepted the job, which soon gave me a sense of fulfillment. As it happened, some managers and sales personnel had begun to branch off from the other two doctors' facilities, and started with their own thing. Through this transitioning process, I began working totally for Dr. Ferrington.

Dagwood Mack, his business manager, played an instrumental role in getting me into the weight loss industry. Jewish by faith, he was five foot five with a medium build, and in general a happy type.

Mack drove a Cadillac®, which he commonly referred to as his "Jewish canoe." He took a liking to me and guided me through two or three job interviews, before hiring me at for a monthly salary of seven hundred dollars as a manager at a small weight loss clinic owned by Dr. Ferrington in Pinellas Park in the Bay Area.

The office promoted a pre-scheduled dieting process, approved by the American Medical Association. In effect, the clinic was selling a vision and a dream to people who were unhappy with their weight. The staff comprised a receptionist, a nurse, and a sales manager.

My first week at the clinic I started to review outstanding accounts established some time before. Detailed records made it clear that this office had operated at a loss. The person I reported to was a woman by the name of Joyce.

Four days after I had started my job, Joyce called me on the phone and said, "Do you realize that you have already doubled and tripled the daily income at your office? How are you doing this?"

"Well, I'm looking at a balance card, and I'm just asking the people for the money, because you said, and they told me at the seminars, that clients couldn't be on the program until it was totally paid for."

Joyce knew just as well as I did that we could also take a deposit from clients, with the balance payable at the orientation conducted by the nurse. I sold clients on the intangible, the principle that they could accomplish their dream.

I became an instrument, making it possible for them to envision their weight loss and to visualize how and when they would achieve this. In my heart and mind I knew it was important for me to be at my best in both appearance and in presentation.

My entire aura became visionary in nature. With clients, whether it was on a one-on-one basis or in a group, a questionnaire proved valuable in determining their goals. Through this process, I created in my mind the best way to reach them.

In those days we did not have computer PowerPoint® systems or charts to show how much weight a potential client could lose over a specific period. Thus, I focused on developing special diets to address their individual problems and ensure they received adequate nutrients.

I developed ways to meet these specific needs, in order for each prospect to achieve his or her dream. This process I developed on my own.

I was tenacious and possessed the ability to quickly come up with a program for each prospect. My first month at the office due to all my hard work I grossed more income than former employees had generated during the entire previous year. My sales totals far surpassed my employer's expectations.

We had a supervisor on our team by the name of Marcus Patel who impressed me as being a poor administrator. My senses told me that this man suffered from severe alcoholism.

Caring for my mother required a considerable amount of my time. However, I made sure to commit one hundred and fifty percent of my efforts to the job. One day my supervisors Patel said to me by phone, "Margie, I'd like to meet with you at the end of the day," Patel said to me by phone. "We need to talk about the clinic."

"Okay," I said, glad that by this time my employer had started paying me a percentage of targeted sales totals, above my base seven hundred dollar monthly salary. This pushed my earnings to one thousand two hundred dollars every four weeks, a respectable sum for the time.

Although stretched in my efforts to care for my mother, whose health had not yet taken the anticipated serious turn, as scheduled I met with Patel in my office. Shortly after arriving, he suggested we hold our meeting over dinner at a lounge in the nearby Pinellas Park shopping center.

As soon as we sat down, Patel started quizzing me on how I made sales and on why I encouraged people to pay their full balances prior to them receiving initial orientation. He began critiquing my management of the clinic's nurse, and started questioning why I changed the filing system that he had previously set up.

I had never realized our employer's company policy would have prohibited me from changing it, but I certainly knew the filing system he originally developed had failed to work for me.

"All I know is, I'm generating money for our company," I said. "And that's my goal."

"Well, you know, you've had to take a lot of time off because of your mother," Patel said. "And we really need somebody there all the time. We think you've done a good job. Thank you for telling me how you've done this, but we're going to have to let you go."

Distraught and eager to vent my frustrations, I called my daddy and told him that I had been fired.

"How much money are you out from not being on your job," daddy asked.

Crying, I responded. "I had been earning twelve hundred dollars per month."

"I can't give you that kind of money," daddy said. "But I need you to be here with your mother."

Once again I found myself without an income in order to help my family. However, it was clear to me that launching innovative weight reduction programs had proven difficult. I felt disappointed, jettisoned from an industry that had given me enough income for at least a little independence.

Karma struck back at Patel when he was fired within a few months. My son remained with his father as I struggled to help my family.

Chapter Twenty-Six

I focused on trying to save my parents' beauty shop located in a San Pablo shopping center, a 10-minute drive from their home. Business had gradually gone downhill and I strived but failed to generate a personal income from the shop. For the moment, I dedicated myself to helping my daddy's business, yet he only gave me an occasional fifty dollars, barely enough to cover gas.

"Now listen," daddy told me one day. "There is a beauty school in Pensacola, named Bjorn's. They have a program whereby after completing a certain number of courses you can work as a beautician's apprentice."

"But how am I going to pay for tuition?" I asked.

"Margie, I'll put up the thousand dollars for you to go do this," he said. "And while attending the school, you can take care of the beauty shop even though it has gone downhill."

I made it clear that becoming a beautician or a cosmetologist had never been among my dreams. Again, though, he stressed the need for me to follow this course of action in order to help the family.

"Then, Margie, when you're at the shop and we get your schedule outlined, and you're cutting or coloring hair, I can pay you a certain percentage of the income you generate," he said.

Again, this struck me as unfair. Nonetheless, I entered classes at Bjorn's, and completed initial introductory courses on theory.

All this while, neither of my brothers came to stay with our mother, or to take her to a seemingly endless number of medical appointments.

My focus remained on gaining independence. 'How am I going to earn some dollars so that at least I can have some gas money?' I wondered.

Eventually during my classes I started cutting or styling hair at work stations. I also practiced on doll heads. I used marketing strategies developed during my modeling career and while in the diet business. Always at the forefront of my mind was the concept of asking clients what they were looking for and ensuring that they got it.

I soon started achieving a degree of success in creating hair styles. My strategy was to handle each job as if it were an audition. Once again I found myself in a profession where success involved something intangible.

Daddy and I recruited a part-time manager for the shop, to help keep the business afloat during my frequent absences. This cleared the way for me to help my mother, while continuing to attend beauty school. Our facility employed three or four women.

Determined to succeed and generate personal income, I started focusing on cutting, the one area where my skill level seemed highest. This proved a key development, since school requirements mandated that I work a minimum number of hours each day.

I set my own appointments with clients, always remembering to schedule their follow-up cuts. I promoted a dream, telling clients at the outset: "This is what you'll look like if I style your hair this way, and this is when you'll have to come back."

This method instilled a sense of beauty in the customer while embedding in their minds the process they would have to follow in order to maintain it. Whenever someone entered the shop, I'd say "Tell me how you want your hair. Do you have a picture? Here is a book showing various styles. This is what I see, and this is what I recommend, and I think it would be stunning on you."

In keeping with the prevalent style of the mid-1970s, I often encouraged young men and teenage boys to get hairstyles with fullness on the forehead.

Adding to my skills, I began coloring hair, and using rollers to set styles. For the most part, though, I focused primarily on cutting since that would generate the most income.

Within a short period of time, I had developed enough expertise that I managed to complete the work at a quick pace, enabling me to personally serve more clients while building my business. I worked under Bonnie Brown, one of my ex-classmates who, like me, also liked horseback riding.

Determined to develop a career of my own, I thought about buying the shop from my daddy but I did not have enough money.

By now my mother was entering the second year of her severe illness. She began to deteriorate rapidly, amid extensive weight loss as her cancer spread. At the time, physicians lacked the effective treatments of today. The high-tech chemotherapy and radiation treatments were simply not yet in place.

Mother experienced the typical symptoms of treatment, such as the burning facial skin to losing quantities of hair almost to the point of baldness.

As an after-effect of my modeling days, I still maintained a very small frame. I had clothes in a back bedroom of my parents' house. My weight often fluctuated ten pounds up or down within three-day periods amid the consequences of my ongoing digestive disorder.

Thus, I kept a variety of clothes in different sizes. My mother did not own outfits in such small sizes herself. She would put on one of my outfits, and then parade around the room saying, "Look. I can fit in this."

Chapter Twenty-Seven

Around this time, one of the owners of the weight control business, Dr. Morton Alvarez, called me, wanting to know the circumstances of my mother's health.

"Margie, I'm coming to the Bay Area, and I'm wondering if you can meet with me." I agreed and we met a few weeks later at a Tampa restaurant.

Around this time I discovered that Dr. Alvarez suffered from severe alcoholism which prohibited him from practicing medicine in a regular medical facility. At dinner, the physician said, "I don't know why Patel let you go. But I want to place you in an office in St. Petersburg that has the potential to be my biggest clinic within the entire Bay Area."

"Excuse me, but I have to call home," I said, interrupting Dr. Alvarez's train of thought. My mother had undergone testing that day and I wanted to know the results. In the phone booth, holding the receiver to my ear, I listened as daddy explained to me that mother's cancer had spread, and that she would survive no more than six or eight months.

"I'd really like to thank you a lot, but I've just been told my mother's condition is terminal" I said to Dr. Alvarez, as soon as I returned to the table.

"Well, you know, I have a hotel room nearby over here on California Street," was his response.

"Oh, that's nice. That means you don't have to drive back late at night," I replied casually. By now I was very good at recognizing when someone was making a pass at me.

Still distraught at the news of the state of my mother's health, and wanting to escape the doctor's advances, I thanked him for dinner and left the restaurant without responding to his job offer.

Within a few weeks my mother's physical condition forced me to stop working at the beauty shop. Soon after, all the beauticians left. Every now and then I continued to visit the facility, answering the phone, arranging appointments for clients who wanted a permanent or a haircut.

Although unlicensed to perform such work myself, I would go to the shop and personally fulfill their requests. I always charged as much as possible and thus, these intermittent jobs enabled me to generate a small amount of spending money. Ultimately, though, I had never graduated from beauty school having been unable to complete the courses.

Sometimes while I worked at the shop, mother would call me, her harsh voice resonating in my ear as she spoke through her device. She would interrupt whatever I was doing with statements such as: "The nurse was mean to me," or "The nurse refused to let me have something."

Whenever mother failed in her attempts to reach my daddy, she begged me to return home. On many occasions I would have to tell her, "Mom, I can't come right now."

I would then ask to speak with the nurse or whatever individual had caused mother's stress at that particular moment, "My mother tells me that she wants to be able to do something."

I then delved into details of each day's specific problems acting as a go-between in order to resolve the situation. My life had become a balancing act of sorts, as I strived to address the problems of everyone around me including those of my parents.

When my mother's illness approached the critical stage, I locked the shop's doors for one final time. I began to spend almost all my time at home with her.

Daddy often left for his work in the late afternoon. He seemed to be on the job around the clock. I often slept on a blanket-covered air mattress on the floor beside my mother's bed. Her ability to speak decreased with each passing day. Whenever she wanted my assistance, she rang a small bell that was kept by the bed.

The day finally came when I had to take her to the hospital for the last time. I will never forget what happened as I prepared to take her from her home. She turned around and I asked, "Ma, what are you doing?"

She looked about the house while saying, "I won't be coming back here."

"Oh, yes you will," I said. "Come on, we've got to go there, and we're going to do whatever they want us to do." I knew, of course, that she was right, but it was not something that I wanted to say out loud, either to her or to myself.

Physicians admitted her to what was then Brookside Hospital in Orlando, Florida. I went daily to see her. She remained hospitalized for a quite a while. Her weight continued to fall and her condition worsened.

Doctors put her on a pain medication referred to at the time as Schlesinger Solution. It was a combination of many types of pain killers and included snake venom. It had a numbing effect on the patient.

While my mother was in hospital, my father underwent several surgeries for his work-related injuries. His room was on the same floor as my mother's. The stress-level factor wore on daddy as he took various painkillers.

One morning, while I stood in a hospital hallway amid infrequent breaks from visiting my parents, a nurse told me some shocking news. She said, "Your father has been making lewd advances at some of the nurses."

Sure enough, when I went to my daddy's room to ask him about it, he started telling me that he had been making advances toward a nurse.

"Yeah!" he said. "Isn't she great!"

Such selfish, immoral behavior struck me as totally out of character.

After the third day of trying to tolerate his ludicrous conduct, I asked him, "Daddy, which nurse is it? Is she buying into this?"

"Oh, yeah-yeah," he said, giving me her name.

Four days after learning of his behavior, I went to the nurse's station. Mentally stretched to the limit, I lacked any clue of what to do or who to speak with. I asked for the nursing supervisor.

I told her of the situation, adding that "I want to have a conversation with this nurse in a private room."

After the supervisor summoned the nurse, we entered a room. Once we were seated, I said to her:, "This information is coming to me from my father. He's telling me that he has made certain suggestive remarks to you, literally overt passes. Is this true?"

"Well, yeah." she answered.

"Look, my mother is down the hall here, and she's dying. Unless you take a firm stand against my dad's advances, I assume he'll continue doing it. His mind is completely turned upside down by the medication and the stress of thinking of my mother's eventual death."

"Yes?"

"He's making phone calls to other women," I said. "If you can't get this situation under control, then I want you to transfer from taking care of my dad because I really don't have time for this."

My strength of character was unleashed fully during this conversation. Needless to say, the nurse relented, promising such behavior would end right away.

Within a few days my mother's condition worsened to the point that death was hovering over her. As our family prepared for the inevitable, doctors released my dad from the hospital. Suffering from severe depression, once at home, he began drinking while taking his painkillers and various other medications.

Amid my almost constant vigil beside my mother's bedside, I made infrequent visits home to care for daddy as well. His increased alcohol consumption was very worrisome. One night, I went into his bedroom. He was lying in bed. I asked him, "Daddy, what is it you want for dinner?"

He immediately started babbling about the topic of sex, adding that "I've explained the birds and the bees to both of your brothers. We've never talked about it, but I can teach you, too. I'm really good."

I stepped back, stunned beyond belief that daddy had made a pass for me. This period was already proving to be an incredibly troubled time in my life, and his bizarre behavior only compounded my mental anguish.

"Come on, honey," he said. "Get into bed with me. Nobody's going to know."

"No," I said. "I'd never do that."

"I'm not your real father, but I am your daddy. It'll all be just between you and me," he said, as I stormed from his bedroom. My immediate inspection of the cupboards revealed he had consumed every drop of alcohol in the home.

The situation continued to worsen until about seven o'clock the next morning when his biological son, Bruce, my half-brother, showed up at the home. Daddy had not slept through the night, reeling from alcohol and pills.

"Bruce, daddy needs to get into the shower, and you're going to have to help him because I can't," I told my half-brother.

Bruce entered daddy's room: "Ah, come on, pops." he said.

A few moments later, I heard the two of them in the bathroom as daddy took a shower. Wanting to know what they were saying, I listened outside thedoor I could hear daddy, "Oh, yeah, your sister would be great stuff. I asked her about going to bed, but promised her that I wouldn't tell anybody."

Daddy kept making similar bizarre statements and Bruce did not make any attempts to change the subject. To this day I do not know what drugs daddy had been taking, but they had truly placed him in a precarious mental state.

Meanwhile, Bubbles Tanner, who worked at a Safeway® as a meat wrapper and who would eventually become daddy's second wife, started calling the house. I answered the phone, unwilling to act in a cordial manner towards her. I refrained from telling her about my daddy's strange behavior.

Daddy refused to listen to my pleas to stop drinking alcohol while taking his medications.

By this point, I had let my hair return to its natural dark color as my meager finances prevented me from the expenditure of bleaching it. In earlier photos of my mother , she looks almost identical to the way I looked at twenty-nine.

To this day I remain convinced that when daddy looked at me, he saw visions of my mother when she was younger, although he had referred to me by name. I also could tell that mother's pending death was taking a horrible toll on him.

Thankfully, daddy stopped drinking alcohol as his dosages of medication decreased. One day, when he was sober again, I told him what he had done.

"I didn't do that." he protested.

"Yes, you did." I confirmed.

Around this time, Safeway® executives planned their annual employee picnic. I encouraged him, "Daddy, just go." During this period mother was slipping in and out of a coma.

Still wary of daddy's behavior, I started keeping my distance from him as much as possible. One day upon returning to the house after running some errands, I found

daddy was writing checks in his office. He looked absolutely drained. I soon found out why. While I had been out my mother had lapsed into a coma and this time the doctors did not think she was going to come out of it.

"Come here," he said, and I walked up to the desk. "I'm sorry. I'm really sorry if I did that."

My grandparents were making frequent visits to the region to visit their dying daughter. Yet dad refused to stock our cupboards with groceries for them. Daddy expected me to buy the food, but that was impossible because I had no income and was not working so that I could stay with my mother for whatever time she had left.

Not wanting to stir anything up, I used much of the fifty dollars gas money he would give me to buy groceries.

While chatting on the phone one day, my daddy let it slip that several years earlier through their employer, he and mother had obtained a five hundred thousand dollar insurance policy on her life. At the time it was an enormous sum.

As I had always stated, in their relationship, my father essentially was a gun and mother served as his bullet. Around this time I realized that in her absence he used me as a proverbial bullet to get the difficult things done, except in a different capacity.

Once she lapsed into a permanent coma, mother's weight dropped dramatically. Adding to the tension between daddy and my mother's parents, my daddy was adamant in his feeling that anyone who visited the house should help buy groceries.

Concerned about the instability of the entire situation, I told my grandmother that Bubbles kept calling my dad. I also relayed to her my fears that the woman would inherit my mother's jewelry.

Although I sensed mother did not know I was there, I went to the hospital to see her as much as possible. Finally, it was time for my family to gather. Everyone was there except for my brothers. I knew this would be mother's last night, but I wanted to leave before my daddy and grandparents returned to the hallway to tell me she was gone. I felt like I just could not do it.

I had been facing the pain for the entire time she was sick, all responsibilities seemingly on my shoulders. I had realized much of my life's dreams before this point, and now I felt grateful that I had been of help to my mother and daddy.

In those days, models on the cusp of thirtieth birthday were considered past their prime and certainly too old to continue modeling. After overcoming the many hurdles that life had thus far placed before me, I had tremendous confidence in myself and in my abilities.

Little did I know that during the next ten years, I would achieve numerous major successes in businesses that many people only dreamed about.

Chapter Twenty-Eight

Soon after mother died, I started dating a very successful man by the name of Al Goldberg. He was from Sarasota.

Within a short period of time, it became a problem for me to remain at my parent's house as Bubbles had started staying there, commuting from Tampa on a regular basis. My daddy and she became lovers immediately after mother died.

I kept my distance but as Bubbles seemed to make my father happy, I just had to accept that was the way it was. I began to think,'How can I move? What can I do?'

I had to decide what to do next with my life. Wanting to clear my thoughts and eager to get away from home, I flew to Las Vegas for a two-day respite. Goldberg had given me a little money for the flight and hotel.

I stayed an extra day and before flying home I called my father from the hotel, "Okay, daddy, you've got to do what you've got to do. My car is at the airport. We can go out and get a Christmas tree, and then decorate it."

"No, that's okay. We already have a tree. Bubbles came over with her kids so we went out and got one and then decorated it," he said.

"Okay," I said, not quite sure how to react. A few days later I returned to the house. tIt seemed obvious that daddy had had plenty of company for the few days I was absent. My main thought was'My mother has only been dead for a few months, and daddy is already involved in a serious relationship.'

It fell on my shoulders to tell my grandparents in Ocoee about my father's hasty decision to remarry shortly after mother's death.

I knew the time had come for me to leave. However, having no money, I needed to ask my daddy for a loan, something I had never done before.

"I need to borrow five hundred from you," I told him. "I would like to be able to leave and find a place of my own."

"Oh, well, I can't afford that." he replied reluctantly.

I could not believe what he was telling me. "You're coming into five hundred thousand dollars, and I gave up everything I owned to come here, lost my house in the process, and you can't loan me five hundred dollars to get back on my feet?"

"Oh, well, okay," he said. "I'll write you out a check. And then you'll pay it back?"

"Yeah, just like I did when I got my first job, and just like I did when I got the car, and just like I did when I got the insurance," I said, before detailing everything I had lost each time I helped him.

What I never told daddy, though, was that with each loss my intuition became stronger, both in the business world and within my own life.

Right after moving to a Bay Area apartment, I contacted Dr. Ferrington's organization, and met again with his business partner, Mack. He liked me, but could tell that I was a still a bit unrefined in business. Yet he recognized the CEO vision in me, for there was neither a job too big to handle nor one so small that it was not important.

As always, the combination of my intuition and my goal of success enabled me to turn any negative into a positive.

I was hired by the Ferrington organization on a temporary basis as they assessed by abilities. They placed me into an Alameda office to see what I could do. I stayed with my friends, Marcie and Doug Whitman.

My relationship with Al Goldberg fell by the wayside. Despite my generally positive attitude, I felt as though I lacked any control over what was happening in my personal life.

'What did I do to deserve this?' I asked myself. 'What did I do? I walked away from a house and I walked away from what was shaping up to be a great modeling career. So far in life, every time I have been in a situation to earn money someone has pulled me away from it.'

Impressed with my high level of sales during my first few months, the Ferrington organization gave me an opportunity to return to Orlando. Little did I know at the time that I had virtually walked into a ticking time bomb of a situation.

The huge responsibilities left me with little option other than to leave my son in the primary custody of his father. As Tim approached his tenth birthday I continued seeing him as much as possible. Thankfully, my father's need for me as a care giver subsided, since by this time he had decided to marry Bubbles.

Working at a feverish pace, I opened seven weight loss clinics in the Orlando area during my first year. Until this point, the Tampa area clinics that Mack managed had always held the company's top position in terms of yearly improvement. This changed dramatically when I increased Orlando sales volumes by one hundred and fifty percent.

His area had already been well established, thereby limiting its annual growth potential and my surge in success became a major coup. Mack expressed his pride in my accomplishments, which had been more difficult to achieve than he knew.

At the time I suffered from a bowel obstruction causing a serious deficiency in vitamin B12, which plays a key role in maintaining normal function of the brain and nervous systems. Physicians had not yet discovered that people with this condition require injections of the vitamin once or twice a month.

As difficult as it was, I forced myself to maintain, as much as possible, an even temperament while critiquing the seven offices, determining and solving problems. My initial annual income hovered around twenty-five thousand dollars, comparable to the base salary plus commissions that I had been earning in the Pinellas Park office.

I worked to build a strong sales team while ensuring that each office complied with American Medical Association regulations, and with what Dr. Ferrington wanted. Hiring nurses became essential, and in some cases I also recruited medical assistants trained to inject pharmaceutical drugs.

As the district manager, I created a position for a licensed Head Nurse for the Orlando Area offices to ensure our company kept an accurate accounting of its drugs and that our medical staff was monitored.

Prior to this period in 1972, I had met Monica Cruz, a Playboy® Magazine centerfold playmate. She and I had developed a strong and lasting personal relationship. It was not until much later that I realized she had used me as a personal errand girl of sorts.

Even so, Monica opened the door to many opportunities for me, including a visit to a centerfold shoot in Miami. The magazine considered me as a centerfold candidate. Meanwhile, my weight loss industry career in Orlando was booming.

Wearing a fitted shirt, tights and stockings, I appeared in one of Monica's Playboy® layouts. However, I was more or less unrecognizable as my head was down placing my face out of view. Even so, I considered such exposure as somewhat of a stepping stone for my budding career.

For awhile Monica kept in regular contact with me, even calling from her poster- signing tours. Around this time she appeared on television with other centerfolds including Shannon Tweed, longtime partner to Gene Simmons of the very popular rock band Kiss.

Monica parlayed such connections to obtain a lucrative, high-profile position as a Playmate® coordinator. This included booking talent for soft-porn films. From my perspective, it was an error on her part to hold a television conference with four or five centerfolds models. I felt it was not in the best interests of the Playboy® Empire

Monica's success was compromised, and my relationship with her began to disintegrate. Our differences intensified when I started dating a former boyfriend of hers, a successful Orlando man by the name of Charles Pennington. Whenever we went out, he spoke only of her.

Through Monica's mother, I let her know that I was dating her ex-boyfriend. After learning this, one evening as I visited Monica at her mother's home, she exploded into a rage, pulling out a kitchen knife and threatening to attack me.

"Margie, get out of here!" Monica screamed. "You've betrayed me!"

Needless to say, this ended our relationship for good.

Unfazed, during my second year managing the Orlando offices, we surpassed first-year sales by eighty-five percent. In contrast, the offices managed by the company's other district manager failed to increase their sales to their previous record.

My duties took me as far away as Tallahassee, over two hundred and fifty miles away and Daytona, over fifty miles away. I taught all my personnel how to increase sales by focusing on helping clients achieve their weight loss dreams.

Without question I had made tremendous professional strides during the first two years after my mother died. Yet, through no fault of my own, my position with the Ferrington organization would soon be jeopardized.

Chapter Twenty-Nine

As weight loss clinics grew in numbers, certain regulations were being put in place by the American Medical Association (AMA) for the first time. The AMA reprimanded Dr. Ferrington for refusing to implement these requirements. By this time, he had one hundred franchise offices.

During my five years with his organization, I noted that the doctor liked to hire people who seemed unconventional, but that he felt had a good grasp of business practices. This he did without conferring with his administrator, Mack.

One day I drove through a blinding rainstorm to a massive Palm Beach estate Dr. Ferrington had purchased with his income generated through the weight loss clinics. Around this time Dr. Ferrington's new associates had convinced him to dismiss me from employment. These associates lacked any idea as to how I had achieved such success.

I had persevered through the difficult period of launching seven successful clinics, making Orlando the company's number one area. It seemed they were envious of my achievements and thus plotted to place their own yes-man in my position. Immediately upon hearing their proposal, Dr. Ferrington told them, "Okay. That sounds good to me. Let's get rid of her."

I contacted Mack immediately after learning of the scheme. As my ally, his initial reaction was one of disappointment, though he was not fully aware of the details. Mack immediately rose to my support. He spoke with Dr. Ferrington, explaining that I had developed the company's most profitable margins.

"Don't listen to those people," Mack told Dr. Ferrington. "I'm telling you, she's positioned to advance far beyond this. These other people won't be able to accomplish what Margie has. Their input would be more negative than anything else, and your profits are going to go down."

To his credit, Dr. Ferrington listened to Mack's reasoning, deciding to keep me on board, at least for the time being. Unfortunately, his managers such as me and Mack were unaware that for the previous nine months Dr. Ferrington had been steadfastly ignoring the rules of AMA.

"It's not necessary to check our clients' urine, or to draw blood," Ferrington stated. He also refused to comply with other mandates issued by the AMA.

Gradually, Mack started informing me of developments, and I truly appreciated his support. Dr. Ferrington's defiance of the AMA soon progressed to the point that the organization began the process of pulling his license to operate a business and to practice medicine.

While all this was going on, Mack had continued planning new clinics in the Tarpon Springs and Southern Florida areas, designated as my future expanded territory.

An administrator suggested to Dr. Ferrington that he transfer the business into the name of a credible licensed doctor. In this manner, the executive assured Ferrington by telling him, "Your business can continue operating until we resolve this dispute with the AMA."

Dr. Ferrington balked at the suggestion, a decision that would eventually lead to the eventual demise of his organization and the loss of my job.

From my point of view, Ferrington's behavior became increasingly bizarre with each passing month. He maintained his longstanding habit of reading at least twenty-two daily newspapers from around the world. His estate had an inordinate number of bathrooms. Hidden video cameras throughout the sprawling home monitored every move of his guests, friends and relatives.

"Dr. Ferrington, how is it that you're able to focus on what happens in different parts of your house?" I asked him one day, while visiting him at the mansion with other managers. "When you're upstairs, and you want to know what's going on downstairs, how can you know what's going on? How do you know if someone is in your cupboards, or going through your papers?"

"Margie, come here and I'll show you," he said, leading me to a room that featured eight television monitors. These screens showed activities going on throughout the estate, including in bedrooms and bathrooms.

This shocked me, especially as his technology truly invaded the privacy of managers visiting overnight, often with their significant others, in order to partake in business meetings. As you can imagine, from that day forward I avoided using the bathrooms in his estate.

Matters worsened. After people had visited, Dr. Ferrington would review surveillance video tapes of their comings and goings at the estate. Adding greatly to the shock was that the vast majority of his guests never knew of existence of the monitors.

Dr. Ferrington made advances towards me as well, casually mentioning, "You know, Margie, when I come to Orlando, I could stay at your house."

"No, Dr. Ferrington," I replied firmly. "We need to concentrate on business matters."

It was certain that Dr. Ferrington was slipping downwards. My disappointment grew when we learned that he had refused to transfer the business into another doctor's name.

The situation became so bad that Mack eventually was unable to diffuse the situation. Things escalated sharply when attorneys notified us that the AMA had begun legal proceedings to shut the clinics.

News of the AMA's investigation and its intent to shut down the Ferrington organization hit the media. I stepped up communication with each of my clinics, to determine if the negative publicity was hurting our bottom line.

Things came to a head when television cameras unexpectedly appeared at my Orlando headquarters. Television reporters started looking for me, eager to interview the district manager. The news media was aware that despite the fact that two weeks earlier the AMA had ordered our clinic doors shut and locked, we had remained open on Dr. Ferrington's orders.

Wary of the media, I refused to respond on camera, simply telling them, "No comment. Go away." Then I called Mack to let him know what had happened.

"The doctor has thought of a way to continue seeing his clients," Mack said. "You know Margie, he really likes you a lot."

"Mack, I'm so tired of hearing that," I said.

"Margie, he wants you to tell employees at all seven of your offices to keep the doors locked. You are then to call patients and tell them that they have to knock on the door to be let them in. That way you're not really open for business."

"Fine. I'll do that." I responded.

Although by this point the AMA had reprimanded Dr. Ferrington, he had not yet lost his license.

The moment my phone conversation with Mack ended, the doctor called, "What I like about you, Margie" he began, "is that you never take 'No' for an answer, and you always get the job done. That's what you do. I know you can do this, and it is going to work. They're not going to take my license."

"Okay."

As a consequence to these developments, the employees began to lose their momentum, afraid that individually and collectively they would find themselves facing legal problems. Admitting to reality, I agreed with them that the 'keep the door locked' strategy had failed from the outset.

Frustrated, I phoned Mack and urged him to call Dr. Ferrington to let him now that the response to his strategy was more negative than anything else and that clients were not going to want to follow these new instructions.

Dr. Ferrington also needed to know that I could not cope with the news media showing up unexpectedly at our various Orlando area locations. As did the employees, I also wanted to avoid being in the news.

"And, Mack, I don't want to make a comment as to whether we're open for business or not." I was not comfortable with that at all.

Initially while working in the Orlando area, I had rented a condo before buying a house on the outskirts of the city. The company's downturn forced me to sell the home, which I did, eighteen months after purchasing it, for a profit of twenty-three thousand dollars.

Shortly before putting it up for sale, damaging stories about the clinic shutdowns and upcoming AMA hearings hit the local news media.

Right after the stories emerged, reporters somehow discovered where I lived and a television camera crew appeared uninvited and unexpected on my front lawn. Once again I refused to comment. I locked my front door, and stayed inside until they left.

Soon afterward, an attorney scheduled a visit to Orlando to speak with me about the AMA's demands. I kept thinking to myself, "Hang on, Margie. Just hang on, and this will all work itself out."

The lawyer spoke about having me appear as a witness for Dr. Ferrington at the hearing. This upsetting suggestion cut me to my soul. The situation put me in a precarious position as I wanted to avoid giving information that was not factual.

A short while later, a received a subpoena requiring me to attend a Tampa hearing organized by AMA officials. It was a scheduled month long period with daily sessions filled with lawyers, doctors, business people, and a mediator. This marked the AMA's final step against Dr. Ferrington.

For nearly four weeks each weekday from nine o'clock in the morning to five o'clock in the afternoon I was required to appear in the hearing room, although I was never called to testify. Two attorneys represented Dr. Ferrington, who arrived on the first day carrying a stack of newspapers.

In my opinion, Dr. Ferrington was so arrogant about the proceedings that he saw them as nothing more than a nuisance. Every day he sat beside his lawyers holding up and reading his newspapers while ignoring the proceedings.

He seemed oblivious to the panel and to its members observing every aspect of his bizarre behavior. To me, Dr. Ferrington seemed totally consumed with himself, as if he were untouchable.

My income plummeted to nothing as I was only paid for generating sales. Having to pay the high gasoline expenses for the daily commute between Orlando and Tampa, a two-hour drive each way, further intensified, my sudden financial problems.

On the last day of hearings, the panel asked Dr. Ferrington to stand up, and to speak on anything he wanted. The doctor's harsh expressions revealed his obvious irritation at being interrupted from reading his newspapers. Throughout the entire month, up until this moment, he had never once focused on the panel.

"Do you have anything to say?" a panelist asked Dr. Ferrington after he stood up.

"Yes, my name is Alfred W. Ferrington, F-E-R-R-I-N-G-T-O-N, just like the famous guitar," he said, his deep voice in a monotone. "And I'm too big. You can't close me."

Even I knew at that moment that Dr. Ferrington had just sealed his own fate. In that instant hundreds of people lost their jobs due to the decision of the panel to issue an instant order to keep his clinics closed and to revoke his license to practice.

This devastated Dr. Ferrington's finances, leaving him penniless. Various landlords ravaged his bank accounts on the weight of fifteen year leases held by his company.

Chapter Thirty

Soon after Ferrington' clinics closed, I received a call from an employment agency. They asked me to refer my two hundred former employees to their firm in order to help these people find jobs.

As for myself, at age thirty-three I found it difficult to find work. I was too old for modeling and at the time there were no weight loss chains of comparable size.

Luckily, Mack called me with good news: "Margie, there's a new weight reduction company, NutriSystem®, being established here in the Bay Area, and I have a friend who knows the man who has purchased a few of these offices. I can get an appointment for you about a job if you can relocate here."

"Sounds great, Mack, I'm looking forward to it, and thank you."

I moved back to the Bay Area from Orlando after selling my home and putting many of my possessions in storage.

The Bay Area NutriSystem® franchise owners already owned car dealerships, and had initially launched weight loss facilities in St. Petersburg. They planned to expand to the Tampa area about the time I returned there. I went to my job interview thinking that they would consider me for area manager.

However, the franchise owner, Charlie Coogan, had already set a specific precedence in building his new corporate infrastructure. I initially met with a young woman who handled interviews. To my disappointment, I discovered they were focusing primarily on managerial candidates who were younger than me.

Charlie wanted me appointed as district manager, but the woman who conducted interviews said, "No, we'll just hire her as a salesperson." Thus, until the Bay Area offices were up and running, I had to commute twenty-four miles from Kissimmee, where I had rented a centrally-located apartment.

I found myself working as a sales person under the direction of Carlotta Southgate, a difficult manager. NutriSystem® avoided giving its clients suppressant pharmaceuticals, like those once administered to Ferrington's customers.

Thin and a slightly taller than I, Carlotta struck me as possessing a high level of insecurity, possibly because she lacked my extensive background and abilities in this industry. Self-centered, she required me to remember that she collected spoons, and ordered me to buy her a souvenir spoon just about everywhere I went.

To make matters worse, immediately before selling a program, Carlotta insisted that I temporarily leave the prospective client in order to confer with her under the guise of ensuring that the proposed sale met with her standards.

This became difficult for me since I had been used to instructing others on how to perform their jobs while also permitting them enough leeway to maintain their concentration amid the sales process. My previous experience taught me that if a customer had budget issues, in order to complete a sale, it was best to negotiate payments with them.

As you might expect, Carlotta's requirement disrupted this vital interaction when I had to interrupt prospective clients, telling them: "Just one more thing. I need to get the scheduling book for orientation. I'll be right back."

From the sales area, I took the paperwork before having to review everything with Carlotta, taking time to explain extensive details to her, while essentially giving customers too much time to think. At this point NutriSystem® charged considerably more than the fees Ferrington had imposed.

Nonetheless, with all I had accomplished and taught to others, I found it easy to ask for the higher amounts from ten to a hundred to a thousand dollars. I achieved success by continuing to focus on the prospective client's dreams, achievable if they followed the program's regime. I always ensured that they clearly envisioned the positive results they sought.

Carlotta's management style emerged as merely a misguided attempt to rattle me. She essentially tried to tell me, "I'm in control, and you're not. I don't care where you came from."

By now blessed with a perennially positive attitude, I persevered through this difficult eight month period until a position for an office manager opened at a relatively small NutriSystem® center in Sarasota.

Upon receiving an offer, I immediately accepted the position, though I knew nothing about the area. I believed that bringing me to Sarasota would give that facility's existing employees greater opportunity to earn more as they would benefit from my extensive sales experience.

Once again I became a sales manager,with a base salary of around one thousand dollars per month. In addition I received a percentage of the income from the sales of all food, programs, and payments which pushed my monthly income to three thousand dollars.

By this point the main corporate NutriSystem® office began hosting annual managers' conventions which usually held in Pennsylvania. The managers would arrive at these elaborate functions wearing their finest jewels, gowns, and black ties. Photographers snapped shots that were displayed on enormous screens for everyone to see.

I enjoyed attending these functions during my three-year stint at the Sarasota office which I was building up into a major sales producer for the company. The center's revenues surged upward under my leadership. My personal income eventually approached five thousand dollars monthly.

Pleased with my performance, Coogan's administrators asked if I would be interested in a sales manager position at a larger center in central Tampa Bay which would naturally increase my income potential. I accepted though some differences soon emerged.

Besides me, the center had a sales clerk, two nurses, and two receptionists. We had quite a number of walk-in customers, and we handled a large volume of telephone calls at this facility which had greater visibility than the Sarasota center.

I quickly discovered how to operate a larger facility, always keeping in mind that the industry's client levels fluctuate year-round, based on the seasonal nature of demand. For instance, many people would only seriously start concentrating on weight loss as the summer season approached.

Seizing on these opportunities, I won a sales contest with the prize being a trip to Mexico. I set aside a bit of money to take my current boyfriend on a one week trip to Las Cruces and Acapulco. Our cabana overlooked the pool and the location afforded spectacular ocean views.

Upon returning to the center, overall sales continued on an upward trend. However, my current area manager and I had differences. She became increasingly insecure, threatened by my more extensive experience. Impressed with my totals, upper management imposed a system that prohibited area managers from terminating my employment.

The company's top executives admired my abilities to sell and to teach. As a result, the regional manager told the area manager that he was not going to terminate my employment, but he was going to transfer me out of the area.

Boosted by the support from top executives, I created my own new position as a motivational speaker and instructor. I held this training position for two years, but quickly became frustrated as the job did not provide me an opportunity for sales commissions, thereby limiting my income.

The digestive condition that had prevented my body from absorbing vital B12 nutrients occasionally triggered an imbalance in my temperament which at times caused me to snap at a salesperson. Eventually, Coogan told me: "Margie, you need to take a break, so we're just going to give you light duty for awhile."

I took this opportunity to take a little time off and rest, and to recover from a serious bout of digestive problems.

Finally, I let Coogan Management know that I was able to resume work. Upon returning, I was given a position as a turn-around manager focusing on centers that were low in sales. I was on a base salary plus a percentage of sales that I personally generated. The company transferred me to various Tampa Bay Area centers that were not doing as well as they should. At each facility, I considerably boosted revenue totals while restructuring its operations to improve efficiency.

By this time I had moved from the apartment in Alameda to a quaint little house in Pensacola. I used the home as a central base, at times commuting as much as sixty-five miles. The modest company travel allowance that I received failed to cover driving expenses.

However, I offset this shortfall by personally generating ample sales. My base salary increased.

Sometimes I worked at a single office for a period of several weeks or at times up to two or three months.

Eventually, I commuted to an office in a prime location that generated astronomical sales totals. The manager there was quite rigid in operations. I seized this opportunity to learn as much as possible. In doing so, I maintained my strategy of focusing on one talented individual wherever I went in order to continue learning.

This helped position me to handle various potentially difficult situations with ease. I found that clients would open up to you if they believed you truly cared about them and what they were thinking.

My determined personality and continuance in learning made me ideally suited as a turn-around manager, a position I enjoyed. Eventually, the company asked me to work at a St. Petersburg Area center, the manager having suddenly walked off the job.

Determined to boost sales, I imposed a Saturday deadline for people to join, in particular for potential clients who had previously visited this center. Some people often visit such facilities just to assess what they are all about and leave without making a purchase.

I made follow-up phone calls. On that Saturday, I lost out on some sales but obtained commitments from others. However, more follow-up would be required in order to solidify deals.

With persistence, I completed six sales on that Saturday, collecting on these new accounts while adding their first and second week food purchases to the total. The average cost of the program at the time ran between six hundred and eight hundred dollars. Including the food purchases on their bill increased this amount by about one hundred and fifty dollars. The fee included the customer's orientation, plus length of time committed to remain on the program, a period calculated by computer.

In large part due to the high-quality of its meals, NutriSystem® quickly emerged as the elite company of the weight loss industry.

Impressed by my sales totals, I began to receive calls from Maureen Blackwell, a vice president at Coogan Management. By this point the area's franchise owner had partitioned the Tampa Bay Area into two and a half districts. I was moved into the district where I managed several centers.

Parking was atrocious in the city of Tampa Bay and this often hampered my ability to sell to new clients there.

My income decreased as individual stores generated fewer clients than in other regions. Managers, noting that my earnings were surpassing theirs and envious of my success, would either changed or refused my pay requests. Yet their efforts would soon prove futile. I ended up surpassing them all as my career skyrocketed.

Chapter Thirty-One

Around the time of my visit with Detective Hernandez, I instigated a major development that eventually garnered nationwide publicity for my case.

After deciding that publicity might help my crusade, I telephoned NBC-TV news in New York City. I chose that media outlet largely on the strength of a positive experience I had with the network in the early 1970s.

Back then, twenty years earlier while working as a NutriSystem® manager at a corporate office on California Street in the Tampa Bay Area, I received a phone call. At this point, I had begun to climb the company's corporate ladder. I was an expert troubleshooter and skilled in increasing efficiency and profits at sales offices, ensuring they were productive.

"I'd like to speak to the manager in charge." said a man in a charming voice, before casually introducing himself. It was Tom Brokaw, an NBC reporter rapidly rising in his profession.

"I'm the area manager," I replied. "How can I help you?"

"We had a call here yesterday from one of your clients." he said

"Oh, okay."

"She's older," he said, giving the person's name. "She has been a client there for a very long time. Have you met this lady?"

"No."

"She called us because she felt that she wouldn't get the proper treatment at your facility," he said.

"Oh." I said, waiting to hear what he had to say next.

"She has just been diagnosed with terminal cancer," Brokaw said, briefly pausing for effect. "This woman feels that, although she loves your food, and she loves the staff, that the money that she spent there should go to her children and grandchildren, but particularly the grandchildren."

"I see." I said. "Now that I think if it, I do know the lady. In fact, I saw her yesterday. But there was no conversation and no request. I had no knowledge of this."

"Apparently she has been on your program a long time," he said. "You know, she really doesn't have any rights to do this. However, she is older, and her condition is terminal. Your business will go on, and she won't. You know, if we ran a story on this, it could be devastating to your business."

"Mr. Brokaw, you don't have to go any further," I said. "I will pull her chart and look at her records. I believe I can get everything taken care of going all the way back to the beginning, including the food and each and every service that she may have paid for. These might consist of food, consultation, her program, and any other purchases that she may have made that we advertise."

In addition, I assured this famed newsman that in order to issue the woman a refund, I could accomplish this task within twenty-four hours, but I added, "I would prefer if you could give me forty-eight hours because I cannot issue a check directly from here. I will notify our corporate office of the situation. I will let them know that with a bit of time I will have a figure for them."

I knew that informing the corporate offices that "Mr. Brokaw would appreciate an overnight delivery would immediately gain the attention of the top executives.

"Now you know, Mr. Brokaw, you did mention that if you ran a story…" I started to say before he interrupted.

"Oh, no, we don't want a story," he said, gently cutting me off.

"Okay, fine," I said. Shortly after this call, I contacted the corporate offices and presented them with the figure in question. They issued a check to the woman in the amount of ten thousand dollars.

However, before hanging up Mr. Brokaw said: "You know, Miss Peterson, you sound like a very bright lady. You're making the right decision."

"Mr. Brokaw, thank you very much. I will take care of this. Now, do you have a hotline or something that you want me to call to let you know when the check is issued, and to where it's going."

"No," he said. "We'll follow up."

"Mr. Brokaw, it has been a pleasure speaking with you."

Needless to say, Mr. Brokaw's professional approach instilled in me a longstanding loyalty for NBC-TV News. In fact, this devotion to the network has lasted many decades.

Recalling my positive experience with Mr. Brokaw, during the last half of 2006, more than one year after the travesty, I decided to contact the network's New York City news division headquarters. Frustrated in my efforts to obtain justice in my case, I decided to go to the press as a last resort.

In this way I hoped to get the attention of someone who could help me pursue the criminal prosecution of Kita Stovall. I chose to contact the New York City office first, as Mr. Brokaw had once worked there.

During my initial call, I spoke with newsroom staffers. I explained basic details, asking "Who do I need to speak with?"

"You need to talk with someone in our Miami Beach office," the reporter said. "I will put you in touch with the investigative executive producer."

"Okay, fine," I said. The reporter immediately transferred my call to the network's affiliate station in Miami Beach.

Within moments I found myself speaking with Fred Morganstein, the investigative executive producer. Mentally stressed, I began rambling non-stop while barely giving the newsman time to speak.

After listening to me, he asked, "Do you have anything to fax me?"

Before our conversation ended, I agreed to send him as much detail as possible. During the next several hours, I sent Morganstein so much information that his fax machine broke down. It was a repeat of what had happened to the police station's fax machine earlier that year. Morganstein called me, pleading: "Don't fax me anymore!"

'Had he gotten the point?' I wondered.

"Did they arrest her, and did they charge her?"

"No."

"I've taken the story into our legal department. You've got something. You've got to stay on it." he told me.

From that point forward, quietly and periodically I would hear from him. At times I would call and ask: "Does this work?" From the fall of 2006 through the summer of 2007, Morganstein remained very helpful, pushing me in the right directions.

He coached me, telling me things like "If this happens, call, and if that happens, call."All this was in order to let me know what journalists considered newsworthy. Things proceeded in this manner until my efforts paid off by generating national news coverage, a public relations coup.

Chapter Thirty-Two

Three years after joining the NutriSystem® team, at the age of thirty-five in 1982, I became aware that my employer had entered the final phase of buying franchise centers in three Midwest states, Kansas, Nebraska, and Iowa. These transactions made Coogan the company's largest franchise holder.

Coogan and Maureen Blackwell, the executive vice president, asked me to become a turn-around manager for these new centers, beginning in Iowa. This began a six-year period in which I served in each of these states, each stretch lasting an average of two years.

Before my arrival in the Midwest, the company had personnel in place there. Starting with the Iowa office, I would remain a few weeks or a month in individual communities. My life became a whirlwind of travel, commuting to the Bay Area to be with my son who by this time was a teenager.

Rather than moving around from state-to-state, I spent an average of two years concentrating on an individual state before progressing to another.

Following six years of these continual moves, I discovered that Coogan was planning the largest franchise purchase in terms of dollars in NutriSystem® history. Coogan agreed to pay Washington state businessman Charlie Waters one million dollars for all franchises in that state and in Idaho. A bachelor, Waters took an interest in me.

Meanwhile, one of the company's former managers from St. Petersburg, Dick Ballentine, a notorious womanizer, transferred to help manage Coogan's new Washington state and Idaho offices.

A young upstart who figured he knew everything, Ballentine would bully women whenever he thought he could get away with it. Conversely, I concentrated on the job at hand, always considering the workplace as a training field, leaving my seal of ultimate professionalism everywhere I had worked.

Ballentine reminded me of the late film and stage star, Sal Mineo. His hair was very black, greasy and curly. He was a good-looking pretty boy who liked to 'dabble the staff', as it were. He would bed with as many of his female co-workers or subordinates as possible.

Without exaggeration, managers from some of our Washington state centers literally lived surrounded by trees. Several of these people walked down dirt roads to get to work.

Once Ballentine arrived in the Evergreen State, he started using the same mode of operation that had gained him an unsavory reputation among the women in Seattle. Although married to a young woman who managed a store there, he literally hopped from bed to bed, engaging in sexual intercourse with various female managers.

Before moving to the Midwest, Ballentine's luck finally ran out when he impregnated one of the company's top managers. She subsequently gave birth to twins.

At the request of Coogan and vice president Maureen Blackwell, I first went to Washington state and Idaho as a regional operations turn-around manager, with a focus on determining the problem spots in a centers and resolving them. This newly created position would eventually place me above area managers, who were not yet in place when I arrived. I also focused on developing this region's corporate structure, while recruiting a nursing director.

Top executives knew that from time to time when pressed on an issue, I might tend to behave abruptly with people. In order to keep such situations in check, the company's top executives encouraged me to take time off for rest whenever I had been working daily for weeks at a stretch.

To be honest, I realized the need for me to battle for the appointment as area director of both states. As you can imagine, my track record with the company garnered me a solid, positive reputation.

Increasingly ambitious, I entered a romantic and sexual affair with Charlie Waters, the former owner of the Washington state and

Idaho franchises, in hopes he would put in a good word for me with executives.

I knew that obtaining the position of district director would mark the biggest move of my career. In all honesty, I also realized that in order to break out above fast-rising younger women in the company, it had become imperative to have someone powerful in my corner.

To me, this affair was a short-term fling, although a key stepping stone in my career. Up to this point, I had never put myself in such a position, but nevertheless, I made the decision to do so.

Eventually, Waters did what I wanted, asking Coogan to appoint me to the top position, although other candidates had been considered. I was now in my late thirties. my son was already a young adult working part-time for United Parcel Service, before landing a good full-time job as a firefighter.

Before the scheduled arrival of Coogan and his wife, Fritzi, I reviewed the Washington state and Idaho franchises in order to develop a chalkboard presentation for the couple. My research indicated that seven offices, some with hitching posts outside their facilities beside dirt roads, collectively employed only thirty people.

For the short-term, the Coogans gave me a respectable title while I occasionally commuted to the Bay Area. I continued to collecting evidence on Ballentine's sexual affairs, since by this point the Coogans had begun considering him for the director post that I coveted.

Partly in an effort to push Ballentine out of the running, I composed a negative personnel report on him criticizing his unprofessional behavior. At the time the company maintained a policy requiring managers to give employees at least three warnings before firing them.

This struck me as paradoxical, since the company had transferred Ballentine to Washington state and Idaho in part to distance him from the women in Orlando that he had harassed.

As one might expect, on the report I prepared on Ballentine irritated him, especially as he had arrived in the region before me. He held the position of manager at one office and his sales record was less than respectable.

Straight away I had noted that he lacked the proper abilities to train personnel. His method of operation was to use his dashing appearance and smooth talk to avoid work responsibilities while continually chasing after women.

Needless to say, my rivalry with Ballentine intensified. Tension started coming to a head shortly after Charlie Waters asked Coogan to promote me. I seized that opportunity to speak with Blackwell, telling her of many reasons management should appoint me.

"I'm a CEO's dream," I told her. "You've learned by now that for me, there is no such thing as 'No,' and no such thing as 'A negative situation that can't be turned around,' and there's definitely no such thing as an eight-hour-a-day job, five days a week."

"Margie, I already..." she started before I interrupted her.

"How many people do you have willing to do whatever it takes to get the job done? That's the bottom line. My personal goal would be in one year that the one million dollars paid for the franchise in addition to all advertising dollars spent are totally recovered, and that the operation in these two states moves into the black."

"But I understand you said something negative about Rosemary," Blackwell said, referring to a cousin of hers who worked at a Washington state office.

"I never said anything bad about Rosemary. I think she's wonderful, but I just don't happen to like her taste in art," I said. "And Maureen, look, you know I had to literally sell myself to her, even though I was good enough to travel back and forth across state and country and up and down the payroll scale."

Despite my efforts, management still refused to accept my conclusion that Ballentine was just not up to par. They knew that I would be willing to stay in order to build the territory.

Fighting for justice as well as the promotion I coveted, I started to build a file loaded with factual information incriminating Ballentine. I felt a need to list the information in such a manner that his termination would be the only possible choice for management.

"I no longer want to be affiliated with the centers," Charlie Waters told me one evening. "They're just using me as an overseer to these properties."

His insightful analysis caused a gain in my respect for Waters, though I still did not feel love for him. In the meantime, Ballentine continued having affairs.

Within six months of starting my file on Ballentine, I had collected enough data to ruin his career at NutriSystem®.

Before long our heated rivalry escalated when he began to keep a file on me as well. By this point I had ended my affair with Charlie Waters, and I had no romantic relationships, confining my romances to weekend getaways, every three months or so with wealthy men who lived elsewhere.

On occasion I needed to stay in various communities for weeks or even months, in order to correct problems at NutriSystem® centers. During these stays, unable to visit the other offices in person, I stayed in touch with them by phone. I made goal-setting and end-of-the-month sales targets primary objectives for all personnel.

While visiting the St. Petersburg regional office for a monthly sales meeting, a colleague informed me that Coogan wanted me remain close to a phone as I could expect a call.

The phone rang as planned during the general sales meeting. I took the call from Coogan and Maureen Blackwell in an adjoining private room.

"Margie, I can't think of a better management person to represent us in the Washington state and Idaho region," he said. "Congratulations. We'll be in touch as to making arrangements to make your stay permanent."

I was so excited that I would have jumped through the phone line and hugged Coogan had it been possible. They promised to send an employment package to me. The salary structure remained low, the same as during my initial work in Washington state and Idaho but by building huge revenues in those states, I could substantially increase my income.

Although disappointed at first, at least Coogan provided me with a company vehicle, a small Chevrolet SUV, something I had never had. My personal car and possessions were en route to Washington state, where I shared a semi-furnished, three-bedroom apartment.

People including Coogan's daughter, Cecile, were continually coming and going from that residence, many of them in regard to NutriSystem® marketing and advertising.

By this time, I had managed to have Ballentine ousted from the organization by submitting my reports along with a very firm recommendation.

At first, after receiving the report, Maureen Blackwell was hesitant to take action. I told her, "Look, Maureen, this is not a threat or whatever. But I'm back here to do a job, to put these offices on their feet, plus add to the region, to say nothing of having to divide my time between two states and three others pushing sales."

"Margie, you've made your feelings known, and…"

"I do not have time to run after a guy who wants to target women who don't know any better."

Ballentine's departure cleared the way for me to recruit the best personnel available, without fear of putting women in positions where he could harass them.

Right away I hired employees throughout the area including two district managers.

While all this was going on, I had started dating a very wealthy man, Bret Halvorson, who owned a spectacular three-level, ten thousand square-foot mansion in the prestigious Indian Hills community, that region's equivalent of Palm Beach. Bret had earned the bulk of his fortune selling condiments to sports stadiums.

The Coogans and he became friends after I introduced them, and the couple subsequently stayed at my boyfriend's home on several of their visits to the region.

On one of these visits, while the Coogans worked to set up corporate offices, I waited in a back office of a NutriSystem® center. I was hoping they would give me news about a promotion or a substantial bonus. Finally, I got tired of waiting and decided to go to the front office to sell memberships.

The center's records indicated eight potential clients had recently received consultations, but none of them had become members. Sharon Spangler, the franchise operations manager, happened to be visiting this center at the time.

Spangler and the Coogans made no attempt to hide the fact they were impressed by this center's efficiency and its respectable revenue totals. That evening Spangler completed one sale of an introductory program for forty-nine dollars plus food expenses of seventy-five dollars.

This left seven potential customers from the list, and I said, "I'll take them all."

With more than ten years in the industry behind me, I had honed my presentation to last between a half hour to a maximum of forty-five minutes. That night I signed all seven prospects, generating eight thousand dollars not including the additional four thousand dollars in food sales.

This marked the first time an office in that area had even approached such revenue totals. Later that night after reviewing this data, Coogan called me at home and said, "Margie, you are Number One."

Within a few weeks he gave me an office on the thirty-second floor of a building that overlooked the skyscraper shown at a distance in the movie "Sleepless in Seattle." If I wanted to see a Seattle Mariners baseball game, all I had to do was open the blinds and look down.

This move marked the first corporate office of my career. As our first anniversary of business in the region approached, the Coogans authorized me to plan an elegant Christmas party.

With the blessing of Mitzi Coogan, I hired a high-level catering service to compose a menu. The Coogans provided me with detailed instructions which were different from requirements that had been passed along by Spangler. These conflicting directives began to diverge sharply. Ultimately, though, the party was very posh and elaborate.

Naturally, I invited the local press to attend. The city's newspaper, the Seattle Post-Intelligencer, published a favorable story. My boyfriend, Bret, shied away from publicity. As for myself, I wanted as much press coverage as possible with the goal of putting the NutriSystem® name into the public eye, in my opinion a key to our success, particularly during the holidays when people have a tendency to gain weight.

I trained sales teams at all my centers to ensure year-round efficientcy which had the effect of boosting the incomes of personnel and causing company revenues to skyrocket.

Under my leadership, the region's first-year sales surpassed one million dollars, recouping the Coogans purchase cost. They also had given me a considerable advertising budget increase for the period which helped bring operations into the black.

My annual income of sixty-five thousand dollars was considered quite respectable for a woman at the time. I had a company car and most of my gasoline was paid for. That helped me to saved as much as possible. I brought my son back to visit me several times and would temporarily put him on the payroll as a stock boy. In addition, I contributed a great deal to his care and that of his stepbrother.

In addition, I still had some money left from the sale of my home near Orlando, plus holding a few stocks.

Soon after my second year in this post, NutriSystem® held another annual managers convention in Pennsylvania. For the first time, the managers from the Washington state and Idaho region were welcome to attend the event.

To me, this increased the importance of female managers presenting an impeccable appearance. This motivated me to personally take care of hair styling and make-up application on the women who would be attending.

By this point, I had decided that I would shortly be leaving the region. Proud of my accomplishments, I wanted to make a statement in terms of my appearance. I encouraged my female managers to dress up more than they were accustomed to.

During my two years in the Washington state and Idaho region, I received three honors including the Idaho Colonel Certificate signed by the Governor of the state. Officials recognized and rewarded my work with law enforcement which entailed developing weight loss programs in Washington state and half the state of Idaho for police officers and their families.

To this day, nearly twenty years later, I still hear from the head of the emergency squad. Whenever I return to the region they are happy to see me. Of course, some of them are now retired.

Chapter Thirty-Three

During the height of my NutriSystem® career, I developed an intense sexual and romantic relationship with Burly Cutterman, a highly successful Australian businessman whom I met while vacationing at an exclusive Las Vegas resort.

For years, every few months I flew to various North American cities for romantic rendezvous' with Burly. Each time he insisted on purchasing for me elegant evening gowns in high-end department stores.

We would then spend several days dining, dancing, seeing shows, traveling around in limos and making love in expensive, ritzy hotel rooms. Our trysts took us to such locations as Chicago, Miami, Dallas, and the Hawaiian Islands.

This was just one of many romantic relationships that I enjoyed with wealthy men during my years before eventually meeting my next husband.

I was not interested in making any type of serious commitment to the men I dated. Instead, I yearned to remain free to pursue a different kind of love, specifically the love of building my life, and my wealth, while steadily improving my ability to deal with people.

The one big love of my life was my son. Through my relationships and my work experience I learned about the things that I needed to do for him.

Through those years many relationships that I initially categorized under romantic love turned out to be mere infatuations. In each instance, I was looking for someone to like me or even possibly love me merely for who I was.

Before leaving NutriSystem®, I experienced for the first time in my life the inklings of the intense and uncomfortable emotion of hate. Since childhood, I have been blessed with the basic nature of giving, either of myself or monetarily.

My feelings of disgust and abhorrence began during my weight loss industry career in the Midwest. It became abundantly clear to me that the only way I could build and grow to care for the love of my life, my son, would be to have relationships outside my world.

At the time, my medical issues were far more serious than I suspected. At times I became incredibly ill when symptoms surfaced.

I distanced my lovers from my professional life and my living environment. As such, my boyfriends never had to encounter or endure my medical issues on an ongoing basis. This lifestyle enabled me to enjoy having fun, while keeping them away from the difficulties of my life.

Chapter Thirty-Four

Shortly after moving back to the Tampa Bay Area from the Washington state Idaho region, I took a leave of absence from work. I was chronically ill as a result of my digestive disorder. Gradually I returned to work undertaking light-duty assignments on a part-time basis.

Coogan called to remind me about the opportunity to manage NutriSystem® franchises he was in the process of buying in Toronto, Canada.

"It's going to be a wonderful experience," Coogan said, explaining that my income would be generated solely from commissions.

"I'm not interested in taking a pay cut." I said, holding my ground.

During the ensuing months, my supervisors made it clear that the company wanted me to return to work full-time, but only if I accepted the pay cut and moved to Toronto. The problem stemmed partly from the Canadian franchise seller's refusal to equally split future expenses with Coogan.

The final straw for me came when Coogan and his new partners refused to pay for my moving expenses.

Although such a job would have been considered an honor by most people, I felt I deserved better compensation and respect from my employers. I made a final decision to turn down the job offer.

Besides which, by this point my illness prevented me from returning to the fast-paced world of the weight loss industry.

This development came as a double blessing. I soon received word that Coogan's franchise regions essentially had too many competitors attempting to establish themselves making it difficult or impossible to open successful, profitable franchises.

Amid, for the first time, an intense increases in competition in the weight loss industry, many NutriSystem® franchise owners found their profits rapidly decreasing. Those such as Coogan who failed to liquidate quickly enough experienced financial disaster.

As owner of the greatest number of franchises, Coogan desperately needed to liquidate his assets the fastest. Coogan owned many facilities stocked with inventory, but he failed to find buyers willing to pay enough for him to recoup his expenses.

Once I learned of these pending troubles, I quickly realized the time had come for me to leave the company for good. It was the wisest move I could make as the sudden onslaught of competition ending up devastating Coogan's finances, leaving him penniless.

Chapter Thirty-Five

Luckily, in 1989 at age forty-two, shortly before leaving NutriSystem®, I had acquired a long-term disability policy to ensure I would have adequate income in the event of a debilitating illness. With the type of policy that I had, in the case of a long-term disability, the holder receives on a yearly basis up until the age of sixty-five, cost of living-adjusted increase based on the month of birth.

I had purchased the policy, initially issued by Prudential®, from the husband of a high-ranking official with Coogan management. This emerged as the best personal financial decision of my life as I became critically disabled two months after transferring back to the Bay Area.

Disability Management Services, Inc., based in Springfield, Massachusetts, subsequently assumed responsibility of issuing me monthly payments.

By the time I reach age sixty-five, my tax-free yearly income from this policy will rise to eighty thousand dollars, plus an additional one-year cost of living increase. At that time, my yearly cost of living increases will stop, although monthly checks will continue to arrive for the rest of my life.

Merely a few months after I obtained the policy, physicians hospitalized me to address severe symptoms stemming from my digestive disorder. My gastroenterologist and other doctors concluded that I would never be able to return to my previous occupation.

This should not be confused with a standard long-term disability policy purchased by the private sector rather than through an employer. Buying into the program at the most fortuitous time emerged as a blessing. I had previously inquired about obtaining such a policy from different insurance companies on several prior occasions.

Partly as a result of having to file for the disability payments at a relatively young age, the application process proved difficult.

From my bed at Summit Hospital in Sarasota, Florida, I telephoned the local Bar Association and explained my situation. For three days, I ate nothing but ice chips. After receiving a referral from the Association, the personal secretary of attorney Thomas Carnes called me at the hospital.

Carnes' employee said he was interested in my case and they agreed to take it on a contingency basis. Mr. Carnes would earn a percentage of my disability income, but only in the event that the legal battle for the payments ended up in court and he emerged successful.

Luckily for me, Prudential® agreed to start making payments after Mr. Carnes provided the company with a completed application and letters from physicians. Thus, I retained full payments and Mr. Carnes never earned a percentage of that income. To his credit, he had worked hard to obtain approval on the first application, and I spent several days reiterating everything that had been submitted in writing.

Tenacious and working in my best interest, Carnes helped process the application in a relatively short period. By the time Prudential® granted the request, the company was three months in arrears in making monthly payments. This income began at three thousand two hundred dollars per month tax-free.

A check for six thousand four hundred dollars arrived in the middle of the third month to cover the insurance company's first two missed payments. Thereafter, for several years whenever somebody from the insurance companies tried to contact me, Mr. Carnes and I remained in communication.

According to Mr. Carnes, this was bravest move he has ever seen.

At age sixty, in the first half of 2008, my monthly checks had nearly doubled to six thousand three hundred dollars. Every six months a physician must complete a questionnaire in regard to any additional problems, along with a statement that they feels the client cannot re-enter their prior occupation.

If I had been hospitalized for a digestive disorder during the five years prior to my trying to sign for the policy, Prudential would not have accepted me. My Sarasota-area gastro doctor had affirmed this when I obtained the policy.

For the first time in the seventeen years I had the policy, Ronald Seymour, the longtime claimant consultant for Disability Management Services, from the Springfield, Massachusetts office recently visited the Reno area. He asked if he could come and see me.

I said, "Yes," and let him know about the doggie bed business, the Production Company and Foundation. I asked, "Am I in violation in any way?"

"No, not at all," he said. As such, the payments continued.

Chapter Thirty-Six

Within two years of leaving NutriSystem®, at age forty-four, I met my second husband on a blind date arranged by my friend Marcia Bloomberg. He was a distant cousin of hers who lived in Lafayette, California.

Marcia's husband, Phillip, was a highly respected California assemblyman who had earned a fortune in real estate. The Bloombergs enjoyed boating near Sanibel Island, Florida, and they often invited me on their yacht.

"I have a cousin who has been a widower for about eight years," Marcia told me casually during one of these excursions. "He doesn't want to get married. He likes to dance, and he likes to go out."

"That sounds great," I replied.

"I can give him your name and number," she said. "He's in the painting business, and he's painting some things for me, so I'll see him soon."

Retired at this point and living on my disability payments, finding a husband or boyfriend was the last thing on my mind. I still lived in a one-bedroom apartment in the Tampa Bay Area and I was quite comfortable there.

One day Marcia's cousin called me: "My name is Lloyd Shepherd, and my cousin a Marcia Bloomberg gave me your name and number." he said by way of introduction.

"Hello, yes, she told me about you." I said.

"I understand that you're single and attractive," was the next thing he said to me.

"Oh, okay. Thank you very much. Yes, I am and I've been retired now for a couple of years now."

We chatted awhile and I told Lloyd that all but a handful of my friends had either married or moved away.

Lloyd told me a little about what he did, downplaying the fact that by this point in his seventies he reigned as one of the Tampa Bay Area's most prominent businessmen. His holdings included a highly successful, extremely profitable flooring company.

His lively voice and cheery vocal inflections made him seem my age or even younger "Miss Peterson, would you like to go out?" he asked.

"Yes, I sure would." I said. I then gave him my address and directions on how to get there. We agreed he would pick me up at six o'clock the following Saturday evening.

"I'm going to take you to Clearwater on the Gulf Coast, on the other side of Tampa," he said.

"Great."

"We're going to a little place called Nick's. Have you ever been there?"

"No, but I look forward to it."

After we agreed that I should wear my normal type of attire, Lloyd insisted that he did not need any more specific directions to my residence: "I've got a map." he said.

"Okay, I'll see you at six o'clock."

Understandably, I became concerned when by six-twenty Saturday evening, he still had not arrived. In accordance to the dress style we had discussed, I had chosen to wear black pants and a silk blouse and had pinned my hair up.

Concerned, I called Lloyd's phone number, but there was no answer.

"All right," I thought. "He's either lost or whatever, but I'll just wait a bit."

Finally, at six-thirty my phone rang. I answered to hear a sheepish voice saying: "I'm lost."

"Where are you?"

"I'm down here close to the Hilltop Mall at the Chevron station."

"I know where that is. What kind of vehicle do you have?"

"It's a silver and blue 1968 Corvette."

"Okay. I'm about five foot six and blonde. I'm wearing a white silk blouse and black flowing pants, very much like the ones that Audrey Hepburn wore. What do you look like?"

"I have a sports jacket on in ultra suede blue. It matches my car. I've got white hair, and I'm kind of trim."

We agreed that I would go to meet him. I hopped into my Mazda RX-7 and drove to where he was. Right after parking, I got out of the car, put my hand on the roof his Corvette, and smiled at him.

He returned the smile.

"Lloyd!" I said. "It's Margie Peterson."

"Hello! What are you going to do with your car?"

"Why don't you follow me back down the road? After I put the ticket in to open the security gate, drive in right behind me and the gate will close. I'll park my car by my apartment."

After arriving at my building, we ended up entering my apartment as I had forgotten something. A moment later, I said, "Shall we go? We can get acquainted along the way."

"That sounds good."

"Isn't it a problem that we're late?"

"I go there a lot." he reassured me.

"You do?"

"It'll be no problem. They'll adjust the reservation for me. One of the reasons I like to go there is that they've always got a band that plays the kind of music that I like to dance to. "Do you like to dance?"

"Yes, I do."

"Well, I sort of like a little of the older type step, not necessarily classical, but pretty much of the big band-era"

"As long as you don't go into the foxtrot, I think I'd probably be able to follow you." I was really looking forward to this evening. He was turning out to be such an interesting person.

The evening flowed like a gentle waterfall softly cascading into a warm, inviting pond. We had a wonderful time getting acquainted, dancing and sharing a few drinks.

From then on Lloyd emerged became a happy part of my life. I started hearing from him daily and we really enjoyed each other's company.

At this point several men of varying ages were pursuing me interesting a romantic sense, most were very successful businessmen. I adored the fact Lloyd always seemed young at heart and that he was always willing to listen to talk about my life and my medical situation.

Eventually, I had to explain to him that disability payments comprised the bulk of my income. He seemed attracted to my passion to succeed, both for my son and for myself. I gave him an honest dissertation of my life without over-complicating details.

At all times, he displayed a deep level of understanding regarding those areas.

Long before marrying Beatrice, his late wife of forty-eight years, Lloyd dropped had out of Sarasota High School and started working to help support his family. Of Irish and English descent, he was the oldest of several siblings, all deceased but him by the time we met. As a young man, Lloyd had gotten part-time jobs standing on street corners selling everything from newspapers to fruit boxes.

Preferring monogamy, his ethics prevented him from dating any woman who would date more than one man at a time.

Lloyd's fortunes grew during World War II, when he obtained work in shipyards painting ships, using skills that his late father passed on to him. During that period, Lloyd took on a partner, Karl Ludenbacher, a friendship that lasted more than sixty-five years.

Eventually the men dissolved their partnership, deciding their friendship was more important than a business arrangement. They had many diverging viewpoints on how to operate their company and did not want this to interfere with their personal bond.

From my perspective, Karl must have been much stronger in his suggestions, thoughts, and strategies. When the men formed their separate companies, Karl's business expanded to much higher levels than Lloyd's.

My new boyfriend's business specialized primarily in commercial and real estate flooring and stonework. He maintained numerous prestigious accounts in addition to jobs on residential properties throughout the state.

I adored Lloyd's genuine little-boy quality, and valued his penchant for monogamy, qualities that I considered very important. Even so, I also knew that for a very long time that Lloyd had maintained a friendship with a woman at Tarpon Springs, where he owned a two-story, shoreline condominium.

At one point Lloyd let it slip that he would see a woman, Marilyn Chalmers, whenever he went to his condo. During our first year of dating, he also shared that while married he enjoyed occasional visits with Chalmers.

Doctors had often hospitalized his wife Beatrice, a heavy smoker, at Florida Medical Center for various ailments including high blood pressure. She preferred a high-sodium diet, and drank large quantities of alcohol.

I took his admissions of a relationship with Chalmers while married as a mild warning sign rather than an overt threat. On the one hand he kept telling me about the importance of monogamy, but on the other hand, while married, seemed to have maintained a fairly lengthy relationship with Chalmers.

My level of concern increased during our first year of dating because Lloyd refused to bring me to Tarpon Springs, which he continued to visit during this time.

'Turn-around is fair play.' I thought. 'I'm not going to put all my eggs in one basket while he's seeing somebody else.'

I still had a close friend, Simon Magilicutti who lived in the Bay Area. He was fairly handsome. Simon and I had enjoyed spending romantic nights together off and on for nearly twenty-five years. At times we would go for a few years without seeing each other and then reunite.

Either Simon would contact me or I would contact him. I always knew our relationship would never amount to anything more than our intermittent encounters.Simon held an excellent position as a top executive for a major corporation. Quite a number of our relatives hoped that eventually Simon and I would marry, but neither of us felt such motivation.

I also maintained a friendship with another man that I will identify here merely as Daniel. We spent quality time together enjoying a non-physical relationship.

The first year after we met Lloyd and I dated steadily. I held off getting into any type of a physical relationship with him for a very long time. When I finally gave in to Lloyd's request for physical intimacy,

I was under the impression that he had ended the relationship with Chalmers.

I did not let Lloyd know that I had been seeing Simon as a lover and Daniel as a friend. I ended those relationships once Lloyd and I became romantic.

Yet several months after our relationship became intimate, I discovered that his bond with Marilyn Chalmers had remained intact all along. This made me feel unappreciated and cheated upon because I had stopped my physical relationship with Simon.

Betrayed, I ended my relationship with Lloyd. He had never thought I would do it. At this point, although he had never let me know his net worth, it was approximately twenty million dollars. Lloyd lived in an older Sarasota home that he and his late wife had owned since the beginning of their marriage.

During the era when Lloyd and Beatrice first married, the home must have been very much in fashion. However, by the time I walked through the front door, the house was severely outdated. I chose never to comment on this. I was more of a listener than anyone ever thought.

"I don't care who you are, or what you've got," I told Lloyd after discovering his infidelity. "I don't believe from where you are, and what we do when we're together that you're only making three thousand dollars a month. Don't give me that; I'm not stupid."

We remained separated a full year. During that period he called me several times, but each time I said, "I'm not interested. Let me know when you want to follow up with what you say."

Ironically, the horrible fire in Sarasota that blackened the nearby Everglades and destroyed many homes brought us together, resulting in our eventual reconciliation.

While driving along a Bay Area freeway, I spotted enormous black smoke clouds and horrific flames shooting skyward from the Sarasota neighborhood where Lloyd lived. Concerned, I became afraid for his safety. I tried to track his whereabouts through his younger son in nearby Apollo Beach.

As flames approached his residence, Lloyd had put on pajamas, made himself a martini, and gotten on top of his old-fashioned shake roof with a garden hose and sprayed the shingles down. Once he finished that, he re-entered the home to make himself another martini.

The lights of his house were on and firefighters and police spotted Lloyd through the windows. They banged on his door, shouting, "You either open up, or we're going to break the door down!" Once Lloyd opened the door, they ordered him to leave the home and go to a shelter as emergency crews were evacuating the neighborhood.

Lloyd complied, driving away in his classic Corvette and leaving behind all his valuable personal possessions. Always tenacious, after officials announced they had the fire under control he left the shelter, climbed a fence that surrounded the community, and entered his home.

This incident served as a perfect example of how Lloyd had lived his life, by his own rules as he saw fit.

During our separation, I maintained my deep feelings of affection for Lloyd. It was the first time in my life that had I experienced the proper type of love to have in a relationship. Before this, I had my share of crushes and infatuations and what I thought was love, but this was truly it. Lloyd possessed old-fashioned qualities, the kind that were significant and I appreciated that.

After I communicated my worries to Lloyd's youngest son, my former boyfriend telephoned me the day after the fire. Speaking from our respective homes, I shared my feelings with him.

"I didn't really appreciate the way you kept seeing that woman at Tarpon Springs," I told him. He acknowledged my feelings, and said he missed me, too. I seized upon this by blurting out, "Well, Lloyd, you know I still have great looking legs."

He chuckled, saying, "Ah, I'm going to have to check them out. What do you think?"

This turning point marked a new beginning for us that eventually led to our engagement, despite certain trials and tribulations emanating from his adult children, particularly his daughter and youngest son.

During our courtship, Lloyd had mentioned marriage numerous times. The idea would surface and then disappear. Therefore, I never addressed it.

On one of our Hawaiian vacations, Lloyd was caught in a downpour while playing golf. He returned to our hotel completely soaking wet shortly before we were to meet two of his sons, one of their wives, and a friend at a restaurant.

Once at the restaurant, Lloyd drank several alcoholic beverages before dinner. As we chatted with his children and his friend, he began referring to me as his wife and told everyone that he wanted to marry me.

"You know, she's going to be your stepmother," he said, looking for the reactions of his daughter-in-law, son, and stepchildren.

The youngest son, Todd, mustering up his courage, leaned over to me and whispered, "Dad doesn't mean it. He has just had too much to drink. He doesn't want to get married."

For months to come, I had to endure situations like this, mild but continual harassment from his adult children.

Near the third anniversary of when we first met, Lloyd finally asked me during dinner at a restaurant one evening: "Margie, what do you want out of our relationship?"

"Lloyd, to tell you the truth, where I am at in my life, I would really like a permanent situation. I would really like to be able to take care of somebody, and to be able to enjoy my son. When my grandchildren start coming along, I would like to be able to enjoy them as well and would like to be able to enjoy you. We're very compatible in so many ways, including our intimacy, and I don't always click with men like this."

"Another thing Lloyd," I continued. "We understand that monogamy is expected for me, as well as for you. We have a nice physical relationship that we're both very comfortable with, and I really do not plan on having anybody else in my life, and I assume that you do not either."

"Therefore, in order for me to go on at this time, with the relationship we have to seriously consider making it permanent. Since that's what you talk about so often if you've had a drink or two, I can only assume that this is really weighing heavily on your mind."

By saying all this, I gave Lloyd a definite alternative because by this point I had gotten tired of being in situations where he referred to me as his wife, and his children's stepmother, when I was not.

"What would happen if I didn't marry you?" Lloyd asked.

"I would resume an active social life. What that means is that, if you call and say, 'Would you like to go to dinner?' I would let you know if I was free or not. However, the physical relationship would have to come to an end."

Two weeks later, during a date, Lloyd said: "Margie, you know I've kind of thought it over, and, yes, you're right. I really like my life with you, but there are going to be problems with my kids and stuff like that."

"Lloyd, I'm not looking to invade your fortune, whatever it may be, but I will tell you that I know it's more than thirty-six thousand dollars a year. I also know that the price commanded for Sarasota's most exclusive homes forty-something years ago, when you and Beatrice bought your house, was substantial. The display of your portfolio as well as mine has to be out on the table. And I will tell you right now, I am not willing to relinquish anything in mine."

Lloyd made it very clear that he did not want anything from my portfolio. He wanted to enhance it, but he also made it known that his total worth would not become mine upon his eventual death after we married.

During the days that followed he disclosed that his annual income from investments alone reached one hundred and fifty thousand dollars. I considered this to be a substantial amount, considering the fact he had already given each of his children the equivalent of five million dollars in assets.

Initially Lloyd proposed giving me a minimum of one million dollars, but then he changed his mind because his children protested.

"Lloyd, whether we decide to marry or not, my income still goes forward, as long as I do not re-enter the weight loss industry," I said. "But I still want to make it clear that none of my portfolio will go to you or to your family."

Lloyd and I came to an understanding, each authorizing a pre-nuptial agreement in which he would buy me a house of my choice during his lifetime valued at a minimum five hundred thousand dollars, or more precisely, of up to six hundred thousand dollars if that total proved necessary for the best investment.

In addition, we agreed that if we separated or divorced before our second anniversary of marriage I would only collect just twenty thousand dollars from him. We also decided that I would receive no additional assets upon his death other than the home, personal possessions that I had brought into the marriage, and gifts he acquired for me such as jewelry.

Lloyd and I married when I was forty-five years old, about one year after we reconciled. Our pre-nuptial agreement stipulated that I could select a home within the Bay Area, with the purchase price as previously agreed upon, as long as the eventual home met my investment criteria.

Hoping for my investment to surge in value on a long-term basis, I sought an up-and-coming community within the overall Bay Area. If I waited until Lloyd died to try to buy a home, my share of his estate would have been limited to the five hundred thousand dollars cash, the equivalent of what he promised to give me for such a property. I looked for a community that would have the biggest growth potential within the next five to ten years.

However, after we had been married more than two years as required by the pre-nuptial agreement, Lloyd reneged on his promise to buy me a home free and clear. He also he balked at putting his house up for sale and dipping into his remaining estate to acquire the money needed for the house.

By this point, Lloyd had signed his late wife's half of the Sarasota home to his three children. He began suggesting that I should be happy with just the remaining half of that house, a value that would only have been three hundred thousand dollars.

"No," I said, and then pushed him to fulfill his agreement. Meantime, I researched the Temple Terrace area north of Tampa, where I found an ideal home with fourteen-foot ceilings in a planned community. The building of a classic, Tiffany's store near that community had not yet started.

Once I selected building styles and features, we went experienced great difficulties getting contractors to fulfill our wishes. I pushed hard to get the work done to my specifications. Finally, we moved into the home during final phases of construction.

At the time I lacked any inkling that within one month of this move, a gunshot blast would blow off the front part of Lloyd's head, killing him.

Chapter Thirty-Seven

We enjoyed a fabulous physical relationship during our first six and a half years of marriage, a dynamic social life, and whirlwind travel that many people can only dream about. Extended vacations brought us great joy, such as shopping Madison Avenue in New York for one week, hopping a jet first-class to Africa, and staying in exotic locations for up to seven weeks at a time.

We also had fun on short excursions to nearby locations including Tarpon Springs and Palm Springs. As a couple we also enjoyed life's simple pleasures, such as barbecues with friends and family. Lloyd belonged to several clubs in addition to his Rotary® activities. We associated with these people at various functions and meetings.

These pleasures made me feel at ease, and for the first time in my life I had found great happiness thanks largely to Lloyd's kindness, love, and giving nature, completed by his excellent ability to listen to me. This marked one of the most joyful times of my life which included giving birth to my son, the births of my grandchildren, and my eventual friendship with Max.

I felt that I had worked hard for the tranquility shared with Lloyd. By this point he suffered from macular degeneration, which seriously deteriorated his eyesight, and an eye specialist had warned him to refrain from driving.

One day, I played golf at Seminole Country Club with girlfriends and then had lunch with them. Upon returning home in Lloyd's two-seater convertible I discovered that he and my car where gone. Driving on a nearby freeway Lloyd's already poor vision was further minimized by the direct sunlight obstructing his view. He crashed into the back of another car, resulting in a six-vehicle accident in which my Mazda was totaled.

Paramedics rushed Lloyd to Highland Hospital. A nurse called me that evening to say: "Mrs. Shepherd, your husband has been admitted to emergency following a serious accident at one o'clock this afternoon. Can you come and get him?"

Tears welled up in my eyes the moment I saw Lloyd in the emergency room. Black and blue bruises covered his head, neck and shoulders. Although Lloyd had worn a seat belt, the impact had thrown him above the steering wheel into the windshield, shattering it.

The wreck totaled my car, which Lloyd replaced by giving me a brand new 1999 Cadillac®. Naturally, this gave me some solace, but worries about his health were far from over. By the time I reached my late forties, Lloyd had crept into his early eighties. He began to suffer heart attacks, failing kidneys, and a malignant tumor on the outside of his stomach.

Dedicated and loyal, I waited on him hand and foot amid his intermittent hospital stays. My responsibilities as a care giver naturally increased with each passing day.

Meantime, Lloyd's children occasionally popped into our home to say hello to their father as I worked round-the-clock to care for him, while also trying to oversee his business affairs, in particularly the dealings required to maintain a large apartment complex that he owned. The stress and intense responsibilities wore me down. I started to look very tired, drawn and haggard.

On one occasion, his middle son, Gordon, visited Lloyd's in his hospital room. He obtained a form of identification from Lloyd in order to be able to draw money from his bank account. Sadly, my husband's children began to fight for his assets, even when he was alive.

Lloyd suffered from numerous ailments afflicting different organs, prompting me to schedule appointments in several communities. His heart specialist practiced in Sarasota, while the kidney and cancer specialists maintained offices in Tampa Bay.

Doctors hospitalized Lloyd to conduct tests when he started to experience difficulty eating and keeping things down. I strictly maintained a list of medications and ensured doctors administered all the right tests.

After not finding anything deemed life threatening, doctors initially began the process of discharging Lloyd, but then I asked them: "What about the stomach issue?"

"We've been thinking his problems stemmed from the heart," one doctor said.

"No, that's not it," I said adamantly. "There is something wrong with his stomach or his digestive area."

At my insistence, the doctors decided to keep Lloyd at John Muir Hospital in Sarasota an additional day to conduct tests on his digestive system. The next day a highly respected oncologist, Dr. Stanton Wilkes, walked into Lloyd's hospital room. While I held my husband's hand, Dr. Wilkes delivered the death blow. They had found a malignancy on the outside of Lloyd's stomach. My husband did not say a word. He just kept looking at the doctor.

"I can buy you five more years of life, at least, maybe more," Dr. Wilkes told Lloyd. "But you will have to go through radiation and chemotherapy treatments."

I looked at Lloyd, who remained quiet, as I asked the doctor pointed questions. I wanted my husband to know what to expect on specific issues such as how sick he would become and how long each treatment would take.

Dr. Wilkes assured Lloyd that his strength would rebound into good health after those treatments, enabling a positive outcome at least for the short-term.

In subsequent days Lloyd told me he intended to undergo the treatments. However, following Lloyd's release from the hospital, without telling me why, he refused to follow the doctor's recommendations.

We returned to our new home, where we had lived less than one month. I scheduled the various dates and appointments to start his radiation treatments, and hired a nurse twice weekly to check on his medications and blood pressure.

Chapter Thirty-Eight

A sudden major development occurred on September 26, 1999. I had scheduled a pedicure that morning for Lloyd, something he always enjoyed, perhaps in part because the young women in Troy's Salon always teased and flirted with him. I thought the change of pace would do him good. While en route, on a main thoroughfare, Lloyd started suffering what we later learned was a severe heart attack.

At the time, though, I thought it was a form of seizure. Lloyd hunched over in the front passenger seat and started drooling.

Unable to just stop in the middle of busy freeway traffic, I tried to hold onto Lloyd and keep him sitting up with my right hand. Lloyd's convulsions intensified. His body buckled and his knees shot up toward my shoulders. At this point, I was driving at nearly sixty miles.

His seat went back into the full reclining position. Miraculously, I managed to keep control of the vehicle, before pulling into the shopping center where Troy's Salon .was located. Desperate for help, I parked in the lot, and jumped out of the car, leaving Lloyd in the vehicle. I ran into the shopping center, and rushed into the salon.

"Quick!" I hollered for help from Danny, the salon owner's son. "Get me some wet towels! My husband is having a seizure!"

I ran back out the salon door and rushed to the car. Beauty technicians followed me through the mall carrying wet towels. I became horrified when discovering that Lloyd had disappeared from our car. He had somehow gotten the car door open, and wandered off.

We frantically looked around for him. Within moments, we spotted him hunched over and drooling on a bench near a curb, eight feet from the vehicle. We wiped his face and neck, removed his shoes, wet his feet and ankles, and rubbed his legs.

"Call an ambulance!" I kept saying.

"No-no-no," Lloyd said, as he started to come around. He began to sit up, but you could see that whatever had happened to him left a devastating effect on him.

We waited there for quite a while in hopes that his condition would improve enough so that we could leave.

"Lloyd," I said. "We're going straight to the hospital to see your heart specialist, Dr. Muir."

Within a few minutes, though, I started heading home after Lloyd consistently refused to go to the doctor. On the way he had started to come around a bit and said, "Look, I'm better. I really don't want to go to the hospital."

"But Lloyd…"

Hearing my protestations, he started to get upset. I worried that in his already stressed state another seizure might be triggered, so I agreed, "Okay, we'll go home. The housekeeper, Tammy, is there. She's helping to put things away. She can help me do that, as well as help me with you, so you will be very closely watched. If it looks like you're starting to have another type of attack, you're going to the hospital, only this time I will be calling an ambulance."

"Okay, all right," he agreed reluctantly.

Once at home, I helped him undress in our bedroom.

"Honey, you take a cool shower," I told him. "It's 105 degrees out."

Naked, Lloyd sat on a seat surrounded by hand rails in our shower stall. He emerged feeling refreshed.

We were still waiting for our new window treatments to arrive so for the moment sheets over the windows in our bedroom blocked the sun. A side door leading to the back porch was open, and I pulled the blankets and the bedspread back.

Lloyd seemed to be feeling better than he had just a half hour earlier. He put on a white T-shirt and I took out his white boxer shorts.

"I feel kind of sick to my stomach," he said.

"There's a medication for that. How about having a little nibble of something with the medication, just a bite or two." I asked him.

"Okay."

I helped Lloyd get into bed and covered him with a sheet, before bringing in a small portion of seedless grapes and half a piece of Oroweat® brown bread with bit of margarine on it, nothing that would stimulate nausea.

I also gave him a stomach medication that I had been using for my digestive problems.

"Lloyd, this is one of the pills that I take, and it's going to make you feel better really quickly." I assured him.

Within several minutes of taking the medication, Lloyd began to feel much better. I turned the television in our bedroom on for him, and switched it to a golfing channel. A few minutes later I went to the kitchen area to explain to our housekeeper, Tammy, what had happened that morning.

"Tammy, I would like to prepare some small, light meals for Mr. Shepherd that I think he will enjoy."

I intended to prepare meals for him similar to my own, excluding his favorites, steaks or red meats of any kind. A while later I returned to our bedroom to check on Lloyd, . He said to me, "Come here. I want you to do something for me."

His speech was more or less normal now. It was almost as if the seizure of that morning had never occurred: "Margie. I want you go to the store. When I got up early this morning, I looked in the refrigerator, and there really wasn't anything in there. We need some groceries. Remember the other night when we were at Kevin and Bonnie's home? We don't have the kind of wine she likes to drink and I'd really like it if you could make me some of those snacks that we like so much, and some other stuff that you think would be good. While you do that, I'm going to take a little nap."

"All right, but first I'm going to have a diet soda with Tammy. I want to go over a few things with her. I'll make a list, and then I'll come in and go over it with you before going to the store. I need to get gas as well."

A half hour later I reviewed the list with Lloyd which included non-sugar, fat-free Popsicles® for him. These alternatives to ice cream and yogurt would comfortably filter through his digestive system. As I began to walk from the room, he said: "Margie, I'm really lucky to have had two women in my life that loved me, and gave me a good life and I have loved those two women unconditionally."

I looked at Lloyd asked him: "Are you trying to tell me something?"

"No. No."

"Okay, I'm going to go. But before I go, can I come over and just kind of cuddle up next to you for a minute, and you put your arm around me?"

"Yes."

Usually, when we did this he always kissed the back of my head, or reached down the back of my neck.

"Do you want anything before I go? A soda or water?" I asked as we snuggled.

"No."

While leaving the room, I turned around to look at him. His head was positioned in at an odd angle, different from the normal posture he held whenever we exchanged an affectionate look. I just figured this change was due to his not feeling one hundred percent well.

"Oh, Margie, I want you to tell me something. You know, I tried to get into your cedar chest the other day and I just couldn't. Do you have the key?"

"No. That cedar chest is old. It used to belong to my mother. Normally if you stick something in where the key goes and turn it around, you can open it."

"Oh," he said his tone high-pitched and cheery. "Okay."

"Why, Lloyd?"

"Oh, I was just wondering. When we were moving stuff in here, I just wanted to see if anything in there was breakable so I was trying to open it to look, that's all."

Lloyd then asked me to kiss him goodbye, and we hugged several moments before I left, heading first to the gas station. I pulled up to a full-service pump at the Chevron Station by the community's supermarket.

As I sat in the driver's seat while an attendant filled the vehicle, three fire trucks, highway patrol cars, local police vehicles, an FBI van, and television remote trucks raced past on the adjoining road. I watched this stream of vehicles, unaware that they were headed to our home. Officials had called every prominent agency available, since Lloyd had reigned as one of the Bay Area's most successful businessmen throughout his life.

"Oh, gosh," I thought. "Some poor person has died."

After filling the car with gas, I entered the supermarket and spent about forty minutes buying groceries. By this point I had been gone from home a little over an hour.

I loaded groceries into our car, anxious to get home to see how Lloyd was feeling. As I pulled up to the gate at the entrance to our exclusive community, I saw emergency vehicles parked on the street outside of our home. Police officers stood guard at a roadblock, preventing me and dozens of onlookers from entering the road.

I stopped at the roadblock. A policeman walked up to my car, and he asked: "Who are you?"

"I'm Mrs. Lloyd Shepherd."

"Would you pull over and get out of the car?"

"Is there something wrong?" A sense of fear was starting to well up in me.

"How many times do I have to tell you, ma'am?" he said. "Pull your car over, and get out "

I said, "Okay," and parked under a nearby tree. It provided the only available shade on this blistering-hot day.

After I got out of the vehicle, the officer told me: "Step over here, please," and he pointed at a place for me to stand. It was by a curb on a very small patch of grass.

"Something has happened," he said.

"Is it Lloyd? Is it Mr. Shepherd?"

"Yes."

"Did Lloyd die?"

"Lloyd committed suicide."

I crumbled to the ground in a state of shock, unable to think, to decide what to do, unable to imagine that with every supportive effort that I had made, being there through everything up to this point—, taking care of Lloyd, and ggoing to the doctordoctors, fighting off his kids, doing anything and everything necessary to protect and care for him, to let him know that he was one hundred percent loved, that this would happen.

The policeman kept me detained outside at the roadblock for more than two hours. He wrote down every word I spoke in terms of what I had done with Lloyd earlier that day.

In the meantime, police had taken Tammy our housekeeper out of the home, and escorted her to the cul-de-sac at the end of the road. There, detectives questioned her for more than two hours. My groceries that were still in the back of the car began to spoil or to thaw. Why this became a major precedence to me at the time, I have no idea, but I kept repeating to the officer, "Everything is defrosted. Everything is ruined."

Eventually, officers allowed Tammy to re-enter the home. The garage door remained open. However, they still refused to let me inside.

Dozens or perhaps even hundreds of people stood up and down the street as Police Commander Delores Sweeny, the highest-ranking official there, conducted the investigation. Finally, officers carried some folding chairs from the garage, and placed them on an entryway leading to the shaded front door.

I sat there alone. The police declined to let Tammy come outside to talk to me. Eventually, one of the officers approached and asked me, "Mrs. Shepherd, is there anybody that you want to call?"

"My father and my son, and Lloyd has three children. We can call them from the cell, but I don't have their numbers."

I told the officer where to find the phone book in the house. He left to retrieve the book and upon his return I asked: "Can you tell me, please, how and where this was done? After everybody goes, is there blood all over the bedroom, or in the living room?"

"That isn't where it happened."

"Well, where?"

"Apparently, after you left your housekeeper asked Mr. Shepherd if he would like something to eat or drink. He told her no and that he was going to get up, put on his robe and go out on the deck.

Tammy had kept the sliding door leading from the bedroom to the back deck open because the air conditioner in our new house still was not working. For the month we had been there, we had done everything possible to create a breeze including using fans in an effort to make it comfortable, given the heat.

Lloyd had put on a blue robe that I had bought for him, and left it untied. A month earlier when we moved Lloyd had told me that he had given his entire set of collector guns to his middle son, Junior.

That statement turned out to be untrue for my husband had secretly kept a .47-caliber Magnum. Unbeknownst to me, Lloyd had earlier placed the weapon underneath the clothes in my cedar chest. After I left that day, before putting on his robe, he had stopped at the cedar chest on the way to the back porch.

The lid was still unlocked so he opened it and rifled through the garments to get the weapon. After tucking it under his robe, he sat on a bench on the back porch by the sliding glass door.

"Tammy!" he summoned her.

She went outside and said, "Yes, Mr. Shepherd?"

"I'd like for you to go into the closet and get my slippers." As requested Tammy went into the closet. When she was reaching for the slippers she heard an enormous boom.

Startled, Tammy ran back out to the deck and found Lloyd. To her horror, this young woman saw that the true love of my life had taken the gun, placed it under his chin and fired.

The bullet exited at the inner portion of Lloyd's eye, taking out that part of his face and head. Blood and brain matter covered the deck.

Chapter Thirty-Nine

Hysterical at the sight of my husband's remains, Tammy had run to the phone, and called 911, rambling while trying to tell the operator what had happened.

Stunned by this revelation, I went through the phone book that the officer had just handed me, and began calling relatives. I was myself beyond the point of hysteria and barely able to speak. After contacting relatives, I told detectives what had transpired that morning.

Amid my overwhelming grief, there in the home that Lloyd and I had shared for such a brief time, I had to account for everything in our past including specific details of when my husband's various illnesses began. It became obvious that the police had questioned Tammy separately from me, to see if our explanations coincided.

Judging by the officers' reactions, it became clear that they felt, at least for the moment, that our stories pointed to suicide. I sat mutely in the living room as coroner's personnel carried Lloyd's remains out in a body bag.

The officers began to leave and they finally removed the roadblock. Tammy stayed with me until my daddy and his wife, Bubbles, arrived. An officer approached me and said, "Mrs. Shepherd there's a cleanup unit that law enforcement uses with murder cases or suicide victims. What they do is come out and clean the area where blood and so on is left."

"Okay, fine," I said. "I don't have cash on me to pay. Can they take a credit card?"

"No, they'll bill you," the officer said, looking at my daddy before telling him: "Sir, why don't you take Mrs. Shepherd someplace and have a drink?"

"Okay," he said.

When the cleanup crew arrived an officer indicated he was going to stay until they were finished. We asked him how long it would take so that we would know when to return. At that point, Police Commander Dolores Sweeny walked up and said to me: "Do not leave town until you are notified."

"Okay," I said. "Is it alright if I go and have a drink or two with my father? We're just going to go down the road here."

"Oh, sure. That will be fine." she said

Daddy took us to a nearby restaurant. It was early evening. We sat at the bar and I had five double martinis. They failed to affect me in the least. My daddy and Bubbles were unaware of the reason that so many law enforcement and fire department personnel had been at our home. I had incorrectly assumed that police had informed my father of my husband's suicide. However, the only thing they had told him was that Lloyd had passed away.

"I don't understand," Bubbles asked me at the bar. "Why were they asking these different questions? Why did they keep you separated from the housekeeper?"

I looked at them and said, "Lloyd committed suicide. Lloyd didn't just die."

By the time we returned to the house, the clean-up crew had completed their job. Daddy asked if I was going to be all right that night.

"Yeah, I have a call into my son."

Tim arrived and visited for a while. He left with the understanding that his wife, Lily, would return to stay with me the following night. That evening I sat alone at home, still completely stunned by the horror of what had transpired just a few hours before.

Something deep inside, I am not sure what, prompted me to turn on the local television news. It seemed instantaneous, although it was more likely some time after I had turned on the television that I heard an anchorman stated that a successful Bay Area businessman, Lloyd

Shepherd, married to a woman thirty-three years his junior, had died of a gunshot wound.

As the newsman said "the investigation is still going on," the screen featured separate side-by-side photos of Lloyd and me. This has been forever locked in my psyche. The media had robbed me of the right to grieeave in private.

Still emotionally numb, unable to cry, I sat alone in the home for most of the following day. I had left messages on the answering machines of Lloyd's relatives, but not one of them bothered to return my calls.

My son's wife, Lily, on maternity leave from her job as a cosmetologist, stayed with me the following night. I was not drinking, eating or in fact, doing anything as all my sensations were numb.

I started calling Lloyd's the offices of Lloyd's doctors to cancel appointments for his scheduled radiation treatments, and follow-up heart and kidney testing.

During the first several days after Lloyd's death, I stayed alone in my room in bed with the television on. Paradoxically, I wanted someone there, but I also preferred to remain alone, gripped with a 'damned-if-you-do, and damned-if-you-don't feeling'.

Long before Lloyd became ill, he had approached me and said: "If something happens to me, I don't want you to have to go through making the arrangements all by yourself. I'd like to go and do that, and pay for it myself."

We went to a mortuary right outside Saint Mary's Cemetery and purchased a cremation and a memorial service. He paid for everything necessary, including the urn.

However, when the time finally came, a problem emerged. A devout Catholic, over the decades Lloyd had painted the Sarasota church for free. Despite this, when he died, the monsignor there declined to honor my husband's wishes for three reasons; because he had married a divorcee, he had married outside the church, and he had committed suicide. Eventually, the priests agreed to hold a church ceremony honoring Lloyd seven days after he died. My husband had made it very clear he did not want his body displayed.

The family ended up scheduling the service past the standard three or four-day waiting period as when his children finally surfaced they expressed unhappiness with the initial arrangements. I accommodated a few changes they requested.

My son knew Lloyd and so he was among those who gave eulogies, including his children and grandchildren. My husband's family refused to let me sit with them, so I sat with mutual friends that we had as a couple.

From that day forward, Lloyd's family and I were on bad terms. Even so, the difficulties involving his death helped make me a stronger person. I became tougher while preparing my heart for the many challenges that were to come.

Chapter Forty

My Yorkshire terrier, Max, stole increasingly large parts of my heart from the moment I brought him home. I had hoped this dog would help fill a void in my life left by Lloyd. My new little friend brought a very rewarding kind of love and companionship.

With all his fluffy hair, he was an endearing little ball of fur. He had the sweetest look on his face and would cheerily tilt his head when anyone was paying attention to him. This made him incredibly adorable to those who met him.

From the day we met my little friend always seemed to speak to me with his eyes. The process of going everywhere him became simplified from the moment we became friends.

Intelligent and ever curious, he learned quickly how to ride in a comfortable, mesh-lined carrier. The design permitted him the ability to breathe and to see outside this container at all times. His comfort and safety zone became my first and foremost concerns.

Max accompanied me everywhere, from doctor's appointments to high-end restaurants to flying inside commercial airline cabins. He often rode with me in other people's vehicles, as well trains and the public transportation buses.

He remained my loyal, constant companion. I desperately needed him during this challenging time in my life.

Before Max's first birthday, a veterinarian diagnosed him with a serious digestive problem, similar in some ways to the affliction I had endured for many years. We both now required special preparation for our meals. With this in common, I felt an even stronger bond to him than when I first brought him into my life. Together we formed a unit, a bond, a team as entrepreneurs.

Besides being my support system in life, Max became the inspiration and mascot for a doggie bed company. Initially, we lived in the Florida home that I had shared with Lloyd.

After purchasing this bundle of joy, my friends and acquaintances started referring to me as "The Lady with Max." He became an instant hit with whomever we encountered. People seemed magnetized by his bubbly personality and his desire to become acquainted with those around him.

Rather than trying to climb up on people like some dogs, Max would use his paw to caress a person's ankle or foot. He would try to stand on his hind legs while gently touching the person.

Max possessed a unique level of delicacy in terms of his presentation and demeanor. Whatever the time of day or evening, whatever the season, Max maintained a regimentary schedule for his favorite activities such as going for walks.

We eventually expanded these strolls into mile long excursions, at least twice daily, intermingled with a shorter walk in the middle of the day. At all times it was important to keep in mind his severe digestive disorder, similar in many ways to that of a person.

All of Max' attributes endeared me to him. He did quite well going into the fourth year following my husband's death, and for the time being my health seemed reasonably stable. As doctors developed special recipes for me, so did veterinarians for Max.

I knew there was a major event in our future, but was not sure what. As our bond increased, I kept a stool for Max at the foot of my bed. By now his weight now up to five or six pounds. He used the stool as a springboard of sorts when bounding up onto my bed.

Max loved coming over and laying on my side of the bed, or crawling up on my pillow. To get comfortable, he used his paws to pull blankets around or above himself so that he could nest on either side of the bed.

Keeping comfortable became important to him. This process no doubt seemed natural as I had raised him to always look for the comfort zone. I had adopted similar behavior during my career which had been enforced even more during my marriage to Lloyd.

After my husband died, I increased my efforts to seek comfort and it seemed that Max had picked up on this behavior.

To me, my little friend was not merely a dog. He became a four-legged person that I cared for, and who cared for me. As time went by, the two of us continued our regime, expanding our adventures to include visiting high-end stores such as Nordstrom's and Macy's.

It reached the point where we occasionally flew from one coast to the other. Since maintaining good health for Max remained a top priority, I consulted his primary internist-veterinarian who provided me with a mild medication for Max, enabling him to sleep.

Thanks to the loving care and exercise I gave Max, he never suffered urinary problems or other issues with his elimination system. I used the finest carrier possible and the best bed cushioning available to ensure his comfort.

Upon waking up, Max would be instantly alert, never appearing to be groggy or drugged. On one occasion as we flew on a commercial airliner, the two seats on my left were unoccupied and I placed his carrier on the furthest seat. I lifted up the armrest bar, and unzipped the opening on Max's carrier.

He sat in his carrier with his paws out, looking at me while cocking his head. Yorkies have a tendency towards hypoglycemia. As such, I always had small amounts of soft or crunchy food available with me.

These treats are excellent as in-between meal snacks. The level of care required increases for tea cupped size Yorkshire terriers weighing four pounds or less. Max was on the higher end of this scale and enjoyed his treats without any problem.

Flight attendants crowded around our seats, everyone thought he was adorable and asked to pet him. They all fell in love with my Max. I heard them say that they did not often have an animal on board who was as well behaved as he was.

Over the years, even before I acquired Max, the airlines had changed their rules and began requiring that pets fly in the cargo holds. A strain like that would have killed Max as he would have succumbed to the severe cold and noisiness of the hold.

While making the decision to get Max, I had foreseen the eventual need for him to travel with me. Friends and animal experts advised me to obtain a letter from one of my physicians, stating the need for him to travel in the passenger area with me.

Whenever making flight reservations I told the clerks or travel agents that Max would be flying with me and informed them of the doctor's letter. Flight crews granted all these requests. It was never a problem.

In the case that I felt that extensive traveling might endanger Max's health or make him uncomfortable, I would hire a nanny to care for him at our home.

Chapter Forty-One

In 2003, I moved with Max to a home I bought in Reno. I was eager for a new environment and determined to end my reclusive lifestyle. Several months after making this move, I drew some rough sketches on a notepad of a high-end doggie bed for Max. I wanted to develop a comfortable, warm design that would convey a bold statement.

The process that began as the simple procedure of designing a single bed ended up developing into a line of similar products. The Yorkshire terrier and another breed, the Silky terrier, both have long hair, all pups are born black and tan, or blue and tan, and their hair at birth is very curly.

These dogs require frequent brushing. Yet the hair sometimes fails to grow well on some of the animals within these breeds. In my opinion, the weather plays the first and foremost factor. Thus, I began designing a cup for Max that became popular with other dog owners.

I felt that in order to make a statement for the doggie beds, Max needed a little glitz.

I started putting a special collar that had a tuxedo bow tie on Max. His leash was accented by glistening rhinestones and I procured for him a vest made from one crystal fox pelt secured with Velcro® Brand Fasteners.

Max was very clever and I never really needed to issue commands to him. Whenever we entered an establishment of someone else's home, I would say, "Now, Max" and he would immediately take the lead. This enabled me to stay in the background, which I always wanted to do in regards to him.

Max began sampling my various doggie bed designs. I would often purchase standard doggie beds and then refashion certain design features. Each time, I carefully observed how Max enjoyed each bed. Through all my work in developing test beds, I finally created a perfect one for extremely hot days.

This new design made it unnecessary for me to remove the cushion from his other bed. Gradually, I laid these various designs out in my home, and Max immediately became my official tester without any prompting on my part.

Encouraged by his behavior, I began to develop an exclusive line of high-end doggie beds, naming them in his honor, Maximize M Doggie Beds.

I provided the artwork, the selection of fabrics, and various types of threads. In many ways my work was similar to that of interior designers. Pleased with my initial creations, I began experimenting with color schemes, sizes and styles.

I had established the company with help from my business advisors and lawyers, several months prior to traveling to Los Angels for my surgeries. In the meantime, I made myself available to Reno area stores and potential buyers giving advice on everything from colors to bed sizes, styles, and where to place the beds.

Max accompanied me on these excursions. It seemed he had an instinct for selling, pulling at the heartstrings of prospective clients. Perhaps he was born with these skills or perhaps he learned them from me.

I know this sounds strange, but to this day I remain convinced at Max took his lead from me. As a team we truly learned from each other.

Whenever someone arrived at our home, Max would jump out of his little house to greet the visitor. He behaved this way as well when I attended formal appointments such as accounting sessions in conference rooms or boardrooms.

I would place his carrier on a table. He would stay inside, sticking his head or his paws outside the opening. If I said to him, for example, something like, "Go talk to Cheryl," he would bound out of his carrier and scurry over to that person.

During visits with potential doggie bed buyers, I would bring in one or two different styles. Invariably, Max would climb on one of the beds and lie still while I completed the sale. At this point his head would be either up or down.

When he lifted his head, his ears would perk up and he would cock his head from side to side, looking simply adorable. People commented admiringly on the fact that he never barked and that he was so well house-trained.

As a marketing expert, I considered this phase to be a regional test of the products. I felt the business had astronomical potential, which unfortunately fell by the wayside, at least temporarily, as a result of the travesty involving the nurse.

During the final months before that fateful trip to Los Angeles, I had begun to research what I needed to do in order to take advantage of the Internet as a publicity tool and in addition, to create a high quality magazine in which to promote the beds and any spin-off products. The travesty caused everything to come to a complete stop. Meanwhile, adding to the already devastating events, within one year after my return from Los Angeles, Max was diagnosed as suffering from a terminal illness.

In Maxmillion Joseph Esquire's short life he provided me with love and contributed so much to my life, and to my desire to go on. His heart was truly that of a Junior CEO, my Little Entrepreneur. Unlike as had many of the people in my life, Max never betrayed me, and remained forever loyal and loving.

He expected no more from me than I expected from him.

Chapter Forty-Two

After more than seven hours of emergency surgery to remove cancer from inside and on top of his liver, Max lay, still alive, in a Bay Area veterinary office recovery room. It was ten minutes past eight o'clock on the morning of December 29, 2006.

Veterinarians and a radiologist had made a series of errors during the previous seventy-two hours. A proper diagnosis earlier on might have saved Max.

While cradling my little friend as he clung to life, I summoned the veterinarian, and said, "His catheter filled with only a small amount of urine, and that's all he's done from the time I walked him. Is there a quick test to see if that kidney is starting to work again?"

"Yes."

"How long does it take?"

"Ten minutes, and we'll have it," he said.

The doctor administered the test which soon showed that the kidney had not started functioning.

"Does he hurt?" I asked, weeping.

"Yes."

"Get the medicine."

Quiet and calm, in as professional manner as possible, the doctor removed a syringe from a nearby cabinet.

I held my dear little Max as the veterinarian started crying.

Tears began streaming down the doctor's cheeks as he walked toward me and Max with the syringe which would end Max' suffering. I knew the doctor had been taught to avoid behaving this way, but his veterinarian's heart got the best of him, to the point that his own deep grief and sadness fully revealed itself.

"Doctor, hurry," I wept softly, speaking in the voice of a little girl. "Hurry, please. Don't let him hurt any more."

Max's eyes closed for the final time after only three seconds, his life suddenly a memory as I burst into tears.

I sat alone in that dark room, holding my lifeless little guy for the next three hours. I refused to allow anyone to take his body from me.

Finally, a woman who had been sitting with me in the surgical facility entered the room and sat next to me.

"Margie," the woman said, her voice kind and as soft. "Come on. Let's take Max, and we'll go over and sit down. I'll show you some things, and you can design and pick what you want."

I told the woman I wanted to cremate Max, so that I could take his remains home to Reno. We walked into a showroom featuring pet funeral supplies, including tiny coffins.

With her assistance, I picked the most appropriate items available. I sat down for a little while longer.

"I would like you to cremate Max with his favorite blanket, and his favorite toy," I said, and they fulfilled my wishes.

A week or so later, I returned to pick up his remains. Everything they did for him had been very kind and thoughtful.

His untimely death put vengeance in my heart, vastly increasing my motivation to have the nurse, Kita Stovall, convicted and punished with a long prison sentence.

Chapter Forty-Three

At the start of 2007, my overall health began to recover somewhat. My new financial advisor, Martha Mitchell, helped me locate where the nineteen thousand dollars had been placed in current Wells Fargo records.

From my viewpoint, the bank protected the nurse by hiding documented proof that the institution had upon request immediately issued Kita Stovall a cashier's check. All the while, Wells Fargo continued to ruin my finances by retaining negative marks on my credit ratings.

Worsening matters, by this point my total financial losses resulting from the travesty approached one million dollars. This had started with the initial loss of twenty-two thousand, three hundred dollars from the two initial checks, followed by legal fees and extensive medical expenses.

During the first few months of the year all my efforts were focused on providing information to Detective Hernandez and the Los Angeles District Attorney's Office.

By this point Wells Fargo Bank had been harassing me for eighteen months amidst the most severe physical illness of my life.

On the positive side, my medical condition had significantly improved. Even so, the overriding need to focus on collecting evidence took me away from my two budding businesses, thereby cutting deeply into my potential income.

Thanks primarily to my relentless tenacity and my new financial advisor, the district attorney decided to change the original charge of fraud against the nurse to embezzlement, thereby clearing the way for potential prosecution.

My excitement reached sky-high levels in August 2007 when Detective Hernandez called me to say that the nurse would be arrested upon the arrival in his office of certain documents from Wells Fargo Bank and that according to the district attorney who filed charges, the nurse would be going to jail.

I told the detective that Wells Fargo Bank had ignored similar written requests in the past, but the detective assured me before we hung up that Wells Fargo would have to comply because it was an order signed by the judge.

The detective never revealed specifics about the requested documents, but he assured me that those papers would result in an arrest and a conviction. This helped put me at ease, since I knew that Wells Fargo had posted Kita Stovall's account number on the back of a cashier's check that she had put my name on.

About three weeks later, at the end of August 2007, Detective Hernandez called me to say, "Margie, I want you to know that Kita Stovall has been arrested."

"Fabulous!"

"Yes, I'll keep you posted, and the charge is grand theft."

Right away, I phoned Fred Morganstein, the investigative executive producer at the NBC-TV affiliate station in Los Angeles.

"Fred, this is Margie Shepherd," I said. "Kita Stovall, the nurse that I told you about, the one I broke your fax machine over, that one, she has been arrested."

"What court?" he asked. "What district attorney? Give it to me. The courthouse is going to close soon for the day."

I gave Morganstein the basic details.

"Margie, it's now a definite story," the producer said. "This is a newsworthy development. We'll be in court at the time of the next hearing. When can you come to Southern California for an interview?"

Morganstein scheduled a time for me to visit his studio in a few months during the time I would be in Los Angeles for a scheduled visit to the doctor's office.

Meanwhile, the detective and the district attorney asked me to avoid attending several court hearings for the nurse that would be held during the next few months.

As the fall of 2007 began, Detective Hernandez called me again, this time to say that a court hearing had been held and that Kita Stovall was going to jail.

Needless to say, I felt vindicated and also satisfied that my hard work had paid off. The detective never revealed whether she had pleaded guilty.

Shortly after receiving this news, I got a call one day from a man who identified himself as a probation officer. He was quite abrupt on the phone as he explained that the nurse would be going to either a city jail or a prison.

The probation officer stated that city jail would be better, because that way Kita Stovall would not have the time she had to serve cut short. He also informed me that if authorities eventually sent her to a prison, she might have up to half of her original sentence commuted reducing her imprisonment before then going on probation.

"What are you looking to get out of this case?" the man grumbled.

"I want her to go to jail," I said. "And if there is a way to get some money or whatever, I would like to go for that as well, but primarily my focus is on jail."

"Okay, fine," he said, before asking a few other quick questions. I had the distinct impression that he had been irritated with me from the beginning of our brief conversation.

Within a week the probation officer called back for a follow-up interview and admitted to me that he had been having a bad day during our original discussion. Nonetheless, I found out that during the nurse's next court appearance officials told her that probation would be considered under 'guarded' circumstances.

A receptionist at the district attorney's office explained to me this meant that sentencing officials had told the judge they were unsure whether the nurse would make a good candidate for parole or probation. I considered this to be excellent news.

Then, I learned that the judge, who had overseen each hearing, had lessened the criminal charge to 'attempted grand theft' because the nurse's attorney had stated to the court: "Ms. Stovall never got anything. And the district attorney's office hasn't produced anything to say that she got any money."

Although the judge lessened the charge, during the hearing he also picked up the bank's surveillance photo showing me with my head bandaged. Upon seeing this, he said, "Something isn't right."

After Kita Stovall pleaded innocent, the sentencing judge decided he wanted more details about the case before making a decision. Thus, by early October, my short-term satisfaction had turned to disappointment. In the meantime, the detective and the district attorney withheld details from me pertaining to the evidence they collected.

My senses told me that these officials had failed to look at specific information that could be used as key evidence, such as the ruination of my line of credit and a new account that Wells Fargo had set up without my permission, in order to transfer my alleged nineteen thousand dollars to the bank into a different set of records.

As far as I could tell, incompetent prosecutors and detectives also apparently failed to subpoena records indicating that Wells Fargo had issued the nurse a check for that amount. As a result, they lacked evidence that could have proven she had gotten the money.

Wells Fargo Bank had sent several written statements and letters to various people who had been looking into the case.

During the first eighteen months since the travesty, while still hoping to resolve this issue, my financial advisor and I kept making good-faith payments to the bank on the alleged nineteen thousand dollar debt that the bank Yet, the bank failed or refused to cooperate with us.

Worsening matters, the bank also had the audacity to tell the detective that I knew exactly what I was doing when Kita Stovall took me into the bank.

Throughout the late summer and early fall, I strived to uncover vital information or evidence that authorities could still subpoena. Through my correspondence and calls to the doctor's office, I discovered that the physician employed an office administrator.

The administrator should have appeared immediately after the travesty rather than two years later. The situation reached a climax in the late summer of 2007 when I telephoned the doctor's office. The receptionist transferred my call to a man who said: "Hello, this is Ron. Can I help you?"

"I've never heard of you. This is Margie Shepherd, and I need to make an appointment with the doctor for something that is growing worse with each passing day. In what capacity do you work at the office?"

"I handle problems when they arise." he answered.

"Oh," I said. "Am I a problem?"

"No," he said. "The doctor likes you, and I like you. Everybody here likes you."

"Really? Ron, are you aware of what happened to me in 2005? Let me go over the events with you."

I heard him sigh and I received the impression that he was thinking, 'Oh no. I don't want to hear about it again.'

My reaction, which I kept to myself, was 'too bad' before telling Ron that from the very beginning, I had stood between various personages of the press and the legal industry and the doctor.

I then proceeded to explain what had happened. Upon hearing these details, the administrator blurted out matter-of-factly that "Well, the nurse was on short notice with the doctor as far as her job was concerned."

"Oh? Why?" This statement certainly piqued my curiosity.

"I don't know if it's because of what happened to you, or if it was a series of things. But I can find out, and I'll tell you."

I might have taken a different outlook from the very beginning had I known that the doctor was on the brink of letting Kita Stovall go as he was disappointed with her inappropriate handling of patients.

Ron never took the time to give me a call back which I found to be quite inconsiderate. He had wanted to get off the telephone while I was speaking to him. I was headstrong and after a day, called him back demanding answers "Ron, why was the nurse about to be fired?"

"The doctor did not like how she dealt with the patients. He said that she had treated them harshly and was unkind. She knew she was about to be fired because on September 1s, the day following your surgery, she called in and quit her job at the office."

"Is that right? So you mean to tell me that for a considerable time prior to my surgery, she was close to being fired and yet she was allowed to take care of me?"

The administrator refused to answer. I told him that I could recall everything that transpired before the surgeries.

Relentless, I also made it clear that Wells Fargo Bank had provided documentation stating that someone other than me, specifically Kita Stovall, had signed the check.

Amazingly, about two years after the travesty, this conversation with Ron jogged my memory and I began to remember more about the nurse, including that she had kept saying to me over and over: "Don't tell Dr. Aronowitz. Don't tell Dr. Aronowitz."

Although I clearly remember her repeating that phrase, I am unable to remember exactly where we were when she said this to me. However, at least Ron admitted that the nurse had been allowed to stay there and to take care of me.

Armed with vital new details, I compiled separate packets of documents and sent them via the detective to him, the district attorney, and even to the judge.

I made it clear that Kita Stovall knew that if Dr. Aronowitz found out that she had left his surgical recovery facility with me, she would have been in a lot of trouble.

With the passage of time I was able to see details more clearly. I recalled being in such a state in the days right after the surgery that if someone had said, "Hey, Margie. Let's climb Mount Fujiyama, and at the top we'll drink a bottle of Jack Daniels®," I would have replied, "Okay!"

In addition, the nurse had supposedly charged me at a rate of one thousand dollars daily for an anticipated nineteen-day period. The question arose as to why she would have required me to pay for it all in advance, never mind the question as to how such a charge was possible in the first place, since I had only been scheduled to stay in Los Angeles for three to five days.

My stay at the hotel had only ended up being fifteen days. I left on the sixteenth day which made several days less than the financial equivalent of what the nurse had bilked me for. Even so, upon speaking with Ron, I reiterated my intention to avoid filing any claim against the doctor.

A few months later, during the fall of 2007, I returned to Dr. Aronowitz for a follow-up visit regarding problems with my breast implants. I wanted to show the doctor how much the area between my breasts had deteriorated since my visit a year earlier so that he could tell me what needed to happen.

The doctor told me that he would have to perform a breast reduction and reconstructive work at the mid-chest. He told me the procedure would leave scars underneath each breast but that the scarring would fade after awhile.

During my most recent visit in 2006, the doctor had told me that my insurance would pay all expenses.

On that earlier visit, in good faith, I had given a five hundred dollar deposit on the total fee of twelve thousand dollars. While still there, I also signed a release authorizing the doctor to send me my medical records but his office never fulfilled the request.

However in the late summer of 2007, Ron subsequently told me that my insurance company, California Blue Shield, would pay for my recovery and surgical suites, but I would be responsible for the doctor's twelve thousand dollar surgical fee.

After speaking with Ron, however, I sent them a fax requesting a refund of my five hundred dollar deposit and once again I asked for copies of my medical records. My letter also stated that I would not be returning to their office, feeling it best to disassociate myself from them.

It must be kept in mind that at the time my former San Francisco attorneys had advised me to sue the doctor and Cedars-Sinai. I was still a wealthy woman and did not feel the need to try to obtain large sums of money from such a professional or major institution.

In addition, the doctor would not be someone against whom I would want to launch legal proceedings, for he too had been duped by the nurse.

This time, immediately after seeing the doctor, various staff members made what I saw as false attempts to gain my favor. They said to me things like "The doctor loves you." or "Oh, we love you' and "You're wonderful Mrs. Shepherd."

Their tactics failed to impress me, especially after the office coordinator demanded that I pay the twelve thousand dollars. The behavior of the staff made me feel humiliated, totally discredited and definitely betrayed. I considered this experience as another attack on my dignity.

It is important to note that what happened to me could have happened to any woman. Aware of the mental anguish and hardship I had undergone, the doctor should have performed the follow-up service for free, apart from what my insurance would have paid.

A short while later, Ron called and left a message on my answering machine, saying, "Margie, what's going on? Give me a call."

Soon afterward, I phoned the office again and explained to Ron why I wanted my five hundred dollars back as soon as possible.

"Margie, I'll give you a refund. It will go out tonight in the mail," he assured me.

Although satisfied with his response, I then stepped things up a notch by recounting details of my personal portfolio, telling him "It was a little more than two million dollars when this travesty began. Does this sound like somebody who wants to take the time to go after a nurse making thirty-five dollars an hour and approach the licensing board to investigate her, because I have nothing else to do, with a portfolio such as mine?"

"No."

"It was never my intention to go after the doctor, despite the issues I had with the breast procedure after the fact. Ron, I'm going to be really clear with you. Because of the travesty that I had, any written correspondence from me was a cry for help, as I continued suffering from post-traumatic stress syndrome."

I then reminded him of many details involving the case. I wanted to prevent anything from being overlooked, while I was also sharing intimate details of my personal finances.

"As far as I'm concerned, the doctor should have dismissed his fees, for whatever the insurance didn't pay, that is, the twelve thousand dollars for the breast reduction," I said, adding that based on my breast size the doctor also should have anticipated the problems that had surfaced as a result of the surgery.

Ron reiterated that he would send me a check for the five hundred dollar refund that night.

"And I can also expect my medical records within this time frame?"

"Yes."

The refund soon arrived, but the records never came and so once again, the medical profession had failed me. A short while later I mailed another request for the records, only to have the doctor's office ignore this as well, despite the fact that every person in the United States of America has a right to his or her own medical data.

Pushed to the brink, I then authorized my Reno-based attorney to seek the documents on my behalf. To our great disappointment, by late 2007, the records had still not arrived.

Essentially, the doctor hade erected a barrier, which I fully intended to tear down in order to obtain justice.

Chapter Forty-Four

During my September 2007 trip to Los Angeles to visit my plastic surgeon for a follow-up appointment, I also stopped by the Los Angeles studio of NBC-TV. Fred Morganstein was continuing to review the case. Investigative producer Morganstein scheduled me for a three-hour taping session in which I was to tell my story.

I continued pressing NBC-TV to consider the various details as they emerged. Despite its efforts, the network never obtained a copy of the nineteen thousand dollar cashier's check.

Cordial and a consummate professional, Morganstein made me feel at ease as his reporter conducted a three-hour, one-on-one videotaped interview. I gave the most truthful and honest answers possible to a variety of questions. Afterward, Morganstein told me that a story would probably air in October or November.

As promised, the network broadcast a five minute story, giving me far more widespread publicity than I had anticipated. The segment aired on the Los Angeles NBC-TV affiliate, and on the network's prestigious program, 'Today Show' which is viewed by millions.

Of course, since the trial had not yet been held, the story by necessity, avoided portraying Kita Stovall as guilty. The segment featured clips from the interview with me and included the vivid surveillance photos.

I felt confident that prosecutors would pay closer attention to this case as a result of this widespread publicity. I phoned Morganstein and left a message to thank him for his professionalism. He later called back and left me a message, indicating his willingness to interview me for follow-up stories if necessary.

Shortly after returning to Reno from this visit, I frantically began scouring documents in hopes of finding further information that would help ensure the nurse's conviction.

To my great disappointment and despite my best efforts, additional setbacks on the case occurred from Halloween through Thanksgiving of 2007. The district attorney and the detective did not provide me with integral details, giving me only bits of information.

The preliminary hearing in a criminal case is probably the most important pre-trial session before a judge. Initially prior to this session, a woman at the district attorney's office had received the packet that I had put together for officials. However, the district attorney handling my case went on vacation as an early December trial date approached.

The person who took over during her absence knew little or nothing about the most integral details. While the person who was to substitute for the district attorney received an itemized index to follow that I provided, as far as I could tell neither the detective nor this new person even bothered to look at it.

Shortly after the preliminary hearing, someone from the district attorney's office informed me by phone that the packet that I had sent had not been looked at. If the officials had gone through the package, they would have found a Wells Fargo transaction sheet listing my line of credit, plus documentation from the same bank concerning the money trail.

To make matters worse, the detective and district attorney failed, refused or neglected to contact me before the initial prosecutor went on vacation. It was shameful that the person temporarily replacing the district attorney lacked any notion as to what was happening.

As a result, as far as I can tell, nothing was explained to the preliminary hearing judge about the transaction sheet, which proved the bank had set up a separate account in my name without my knowledge. Nor was anything explained about the cashier's check.

When the prosecutor returned from vacation, less than a week or so before the scheduled trial, my financial advisor attempted to call her in order to bring her up to date on key issues.

In an apparent attempt to cover her tracks, the prosecutor told my financial advisor that if the package had arrived sooner, there would not be a trial by jury and added she had doubts as to whether the case would go forward at all.

My advisor suggested listing the information at the next hearing, but was told by the prosecutor that they could not do that. She insisted that the only way the case could be presented at this point was in a jury trial."

This left no other avenue. In addition, the prosecutor had no idea that I had been sent a subpoena to appear in court in mid-November. The document listed a number for me to call, which I phoned from my daddy's house in Florida.

Bureaucrats transferred my call through a maze of numbers, until I finally reached a prosecutor who said to me: "Mrs. Shepherd, I don't know why you were sent a subpoena. I don't even know who sent it."

"Excuse me? You don't?" Needless to say, this surprised me somewhat.   "Well, you know, I do have a question for you."

"Fine. What is it?"

Straight away I should have taken her quizzical behavior as a warning sign that prosecutors had failed to understand what they were looking at, or I should have understood that they had never bothered to look at the document.

Furthermore, if she had been unable to find the package, all she would have to do was call the detective. If she had bothered to review the transaction sheet, she would have noted the two columns that needed to be added up.

One line listed the principle payments the document claimed I owned to Wells Fargo, and the other listed the interest payments, for the entire time that nineteen thousand dollars was being paid off, beginning from when the bank put this amount onto my line of credit. These totals continued up to the time the financial institution stopped coming after me for the payments and listed the balance as a bad debt.

Still on the phone with the prosecutor, I provided a brief summary of items I felt she needed to help prove her case including the casher's check, a review of my line of credit and payments to the bank, plus what the nurse had received.

"We're approaching the million-dollar mark in my losses," I said. "Does the nurse have a million plus? I don't think so. And what do I have to get out of this?"

"You tell me."

"A win on this, to a large extent, totally discredits Wells Fargo."

"Well, yes," she said. "Where do you think you're going to get a million dollars?"

"Certainly not from your case, and all we need is a win in proving that the nurse got the money. You totally discredit both her and her attorney. I would bet that her attorney has not subpoenaed for a line of credit. After a win in this, I could retain the best civil attorney in Los Angeles to go after Wells Fargo."

I then briefly summarized my distinguished career for the prosecutor and told her, "Believe me, if the court sees the information that I've provided to your office, you've got her."

"I see," she said. "Okay. You know what I'm going to do. Now, I'm not making any promises, Margie."

"Yes?"

"But I'm going to go in and see the boss, Gregory DeNiro, and I'm going to take the case," she said. "We're going to talk about it, and I'll let you know in plenty of time. Now, I think it might just go forward, but no promises. I'll get back to you."

"Oh, I have a question. Is that DeNiro in your office the boss, and is he related to the famous actor?"

"No, DeNiro is not my direct boss, and no, he's not related to the actor, though he looks a bit like him."

"Oh, he's a supervisor?"

"Yes and no. He's a supervisor, but not mine."

"Then who are you speaking of?"

"I'm talking about the actual district attorney, the elected person."

After this conversation, it was a while before the prosecutor contacted me again. Finally, I received a mailed notice stating that certain documents were being subpoenaed, but none of those items were to come from me. Thus, at this point the situation emerged into a waiting game.

Detective Hernandez eventually called me. "Margie, I have some questions."

"Fire away."

"Was this a business deal?"

"No, detective, I told you, I did not see that check. I have no knowledge of being in the bank, and I have no knowledge of anything other than what's in my check registry. The fraudulent amount is scribbled out in Kita Stovall's handwriting, not mine, and this was not noticed until sometime later by me and by bank personnel."

"Now is the time to say if it was a business deal, and if that was the case we can cancel it," the detective said.

"It is not the time. I have no knowledge of doing so," I said. "To the best of my knowledge, I never entered into such a relationship."

"You can't say that."

"I can't say that? Why not? I was drugged. I've had eleven surgeries in my life, and have been given Demerol, morphine and other concoctions throughout the years, and yet I never suffered through a problem of this type anywhere along the way in the last forty years."

"What if we do subpoena the documents regarding the line of credit, the transaction sheet, and the cashier's check?" he asked. "What if they don't come in? Then what?"

"Then what?" I said. "We go forward."

This was my way of telling him that if prosecutors brought me to Los Angeles, I would get on the witness stand and tell my story. After all, the judge had said, "Something is missing."

I then told the detective of my decision to disassociate myself with the doctor's office. After being cordial in the past, Detective Hernandez now began to act as if he were disgusted with me for telling him that the doctor had never admitted to anything about what I stated had happened in his facility.

"Oh, really," I said, when the detective made his disgust clear. "Well, then, let's just get the affidavit that goes in the black case, because I'm going to Los Angeles. That's it, if this case doesn't go forward, I'm going to Los Angeles. Then they will have a force to reckon with like they've never seen."

"Listen, Margie, I…"

"Detective, I've had it after two and a half years. The invasion of my personal life and my financial portfolio has devastated my family, including my son, his children, his wife, and my father, who is dealing with certain medical issues. These people have looked to me for financial assistance, and believe me, I didn't inherit it."

"Margie, hear this. Only one person can do the investigating. It's either going to be you or me."

"Hey, let it be you," I said, while mumbling under my breath: "Will you hurry up and subpoena the damn records?"

"Well, that other thirty-three hundred dollar check, I'm sitting here holding it," he said.

"Are you really? That's the one right above the nineteen thousand dollar fraudulent check listed in my registry, the one it was determined that Kita Stovall wrote, because it's not my handwriting. And she made the thirty-three hundred dollar check out to a nursing service that I know nothing about. My fiduciary, one of my longtime attorneys and my financial advisor had all individually but unsuccessfully tried to obtain the check you're holding now. And later on, detective, I tried to do the same, and the only thing we could come up with, was that it never hit the bank, otherwise we would have had a notice about a bad check. We never got it."

"Well, I'm holding a copy of it."

"Why don't you fax me a copy, Detective Hernandez?"

He quickly changed the subject, promising to call me back later with more questions.

Chapter Forty-Five

As you can imagine, I spent that entire night going through all my papers to ensure that nothing had been forgotten and to make sure that I had told the truth all along. I wanted to avoid any misunderstanding.

I located four to six pieces of paper that Detective Donaldson had given to Detective Hernandez early in the investigation. Some of these documents had been in the package that I sent to the detectives.

At quarter to seven the next morning, I phoned Detective Hernandez who had just started his shift. The best time to catch investigators is during their first coffee of the day while they shuffle through paperwork. By this point I had become well aware that I was not the first person in the day the detective to speak with.

Obviously, to this point a lot of things failed to fall into place, even after the district attorney authorized the arrest. I remained determined to prevent this case from slipping through the cracks.

"Hello," he answered, his deep voice had a groggy edge to it.

"Detective Hernandez, this is Margie Shepherd. You don't sound very good today."

"I have a cold."

"Detective, try hot water with lemon, and put a little honey in there."

"Oh, yeah, I'm doing that."

"Good, because you're going to really be in a good frame of mind with what I'm going to tell you."

"What's that?"

"Number one, I'm holding a copy of the nineteen thousand dollar check. And this particular copy is of both the front and back of the check, along with Kita Stovall's bank account number. On the second of September is when she was in Wells Fargo Bank. She received a cashier's check and that was when she made a deposit into her own Wells Fargo account. She wrote a number of checks, but did not stay there to cash them. It is my suspicion based on the affidavit from the limo driver that she has an account with Wellington Mutual."

I explained that the nurse had given the driver the address, and that I suspected that was where she eventually went to cash the check.

"Detective, this might be the number one thing that you want to look at. Another thing on the copy of that check, and I know you have a copy of it, because you received it directly from me when I met you in Los Angeles, on the lower part of that page it states that it is not my signature on the pass-line. tIt also shows the in-house Web linking that you would be able to go onto to compare my handwriting with the back of Kita Stovall's check."

In addition, I urged the detective to review letters detailing how Wells Fargo had pursued me. Once again, I reiterated that he could review two columns on the transaction report that detailed my line of credit. This total was over four thousand three hundred dollars, including principle and interest that I actually paid out.

"In another letter from a different attorney, I was advised that I was not at fault It falls on Kita Stovall, and the bank should be looking at her, not me, based on the fact a Wells Fargo employee validated my signature," I said. "But again, Wells Fargo is such a large institution that the right hand doesn't know what the left hand is doing."

I also suggested that Detective Hernandez review various communications from South Dakota, to Palm Beach and to Reno, all of it pointing to Kita Stovall.

To top this off, I told Detective Hernandez about a subpoena that I received in the mail two days before this conversation along with a cover letter from Wells Fargo.

"It was from the bank's subpoena department," I said. "I called the bank, and I questioned a woman there about this particular document to ensure I had a clear understanding of it.

"She gave me the number listed in the document which was that of my checking account," I said, "but the record of Kita Stovall's embezzlement isn't in my checking account. The travesty is in the line of credit that the bank re-established after they closed my checking account and a line of credit that had been tied into it at the time.

"It is on a charge card. Since the financing of my home and other things were not tied into my line of credit with the checking account in question, they had no idea how to tie it into my home. Therefore, they established an additional line of credit without notifying us that they had done so. The account numbers started showing up on the letters coming from Wells Fargo during the time I was being harassed."

Without giving the detective a chance to interrupt, I went on to explain that I had asked the woman on the phone: "In this subpoena, can you tell me, please, since it is my checking account that is being subpoenaed, the way that it is written up, is it going to be an automatic assumption that they will attach my line of credit and send a copy of that? For example, a transaction sheet, or details from August leading into the days before the surgery, the day thereafter, and the days to follow?"

"No," she said. "That has to be requested totally separately, because it's not tied into the checking account. It's a completely separate charge card."

This struck me as interesting since I now have no checking account whatsoever with Wells Fargo.

"Like the detectives and the prosecutor, the attorney representing Kita Stovall didn't get this either," I said. "And my line of credit, he is not going to get."

"It sounds like he went about it the right way," Detective Hernandez said.

"I guess he did according to the subpoena department," I said. "But the bottom line is, I'm not questioning whether he did it correctly as to me that's totally irrelevant. Maybe to you and to the district attorney it's not, because you can build a case around that, but that's not the real case. The case is that she forged my name. And because I had money, and she didn't, the bank went after me. That was the reasoning that was given in a letter by Mr. Thomas Carnes, my former head legal counsel that I had retained for sixteen years."

I now wanted to get everything off my chest I told the detective that to discredit Kita Stovall and her attorney, all he had to do was to prove that she had received the money and further stated that the information had been given to him."

"Margie, I'll call the district attorney and see where things stand and what has come in and then I'll get back to you," he said. "You know, we did subpoena some additional records from the bank."

"Okay, fine," I said, deciding to try to dig for details with my following question. "But Detective Hernandez, when I asked the woman in the subpoena department, I said, 'Amy, can you tell me, has anybody subpoenaed my line of credit in the last six months?' And she said, 'No, it hasn't been subpoenaed.'"

Hearing this, Detective Hernandez very quickly said: "Now, you would never know if a law enforcement office such as mine or the district attorney's office would be subpoenaing certain records."

"Oh, all right," I said, letting it go, taking his statement to mean that detectives had done what I said, and that they would be prepared for trial. "Detective Hernandez, yesterday you mentioned that thirty-three hundred dollar check?"

"Yes."

"I didn't see that check, and I didn't see the check for nineteen thousand dollars either," I said, reiterating that many people including myself had tried to locate it. "And we tried to locate the nursing care business. Where is it?"

I yearned for these details. I still had the business card I had found in my hotel room, listing the nurse as an employee in the Hospital Emergency Room. She also could have been a part-time employee through an agency. In my research as well as that of my financial advisor, there was never any evidence found of the check for three thousand three hundred dollars being deposited, returned as a bad check, nothing at all.

"Detective, you know, I mentioned that three thousand three hundred dollar check when I came down to meet you, and I showed it to you on the check registry. And I told you then, 'I never saw it, I don't know where it went, and nobody knew where it was. It was suspected to have just been voided out.'

"I approached you with that then, and I'm telling you now. Nobody knows any more about that check now than before. So I'll tell you what, why don't you fax me a copy of it, so that I can see the handwriting."

"Oh, well, you know the whole lower half of the page is black," he said. "You wouldn't be able to see the lower half of the page, so, no it really wouldn't be a good idea. I can't fax it to you."

"Whether the lower part of the page is blacked out or not has nothing to do with the copy of the check," I said. "I don't care if the rest of the page is black. All I want to do is see the check. It is my full belief and suspicion that the check is mentioned."

I suspected that perhaps the nurse's attorney might have contacted the detective to discuss the check.

At one point I told Detective Hernandez that I had recently gotten my name listed in the Nevada business directory.

"I'd like to see that, Margie, to learn how you're going to remake your money."

I briefly described launching a motorcycle poster business six months earlier at the beginning of summer. As the conversation ended, Detective Hernandez suggested that I send him one of the posters. However, as he had upset me, I never did.

Within the next few weeks, Detective Hernandez showed his true colors. He never got back to me which I felt was highly unprofessional. Our previous conversation marked the last time I ever spoke to him and it was my final contact with anyone from Los Angeles other than journalists before the trial date. Several weeks before the scheduled selection of a jury, Morganstein's reporter at NBC-TV copied some of the detective's behavior, giving me an excuse as to why they weren't able to fax the check to me.

I wondered why, if there was really a concern, that I knowingly wrote bad checks, they would not fax a copy to me? Why did it not show up on what we received as a returned check? I believe that possibly the check does not even exist anymore. This had been suspected from the start as my checkbook register has a line through that record.

At this point, I became resigned to the fact that I would never know the truth about this particular check, until after I reviewed results from the upcoming trial records.

In summary, as the trial approached, I determined that the district attorney and the detective would be able to convict the nurse if they subpoenaed the cashier's check, along with documentation on my line of credit that the bank had established without my knowledge.

Another subpoena arrived by mail, this time for me to appear at Kita Stovall's trial. I called the district attorney's office, which confirmed jury selection was to begin on Monday, December 3, 2007. An official told me that I might not have to appear at all, but if that became necessary prosecutors likely would summon me the following week.

Chapter Forty-Six

I celebrated Thanksgiving week of 2007 with my father in his Tampa Bay Area home. I was now concerned by Detective Hernandez's emerging attitude, which I found quite disagreeable. Prosecutors had already assured me that jury selection in Los Angeles would begin as scheduled within the second week of December.

The district attorney's office also notified me that they might not need me to testify, though I felt ready for that possibility. More than ever, the very fiber of my being yearned for nurse Kita Stovall to receive the justice she deserved.

Back at my home in Reno, I spent much of the week before the scheduled trial talking with a few friends about the case. Just speaking in detail about these troubles from the previous two and a half years gave me at least some sense of relief.

For the most part, though, I became even more reclusive. Except for a handful of phone chats regarding business matters, I occasionally would go for a few days at a time without speaking with anyone.

The realization gradually came that the entire travesty had changed me as a person, leaving my heart and soul bruised and battered. Although still energetic and possessing a positive attitude, for the first time in my adult life I began to feel at least, for the time being, a feeling of negativity about the world.

This evolution made sense to me, because after all I had been failed by the legal profession, financial experts, and the medical industry, all of them institutions that Americans should be able to look to for support.

With my personal finances now in shambles, my credit rating ruined, both of my once budding businesses remained on the back burner. Although my overall health had improved somewhat during 2007, my lack of funds prevented me from giving my relatives the financial assistance that they had come to look forward to in the past.

During the last few days of November and through the first weekend of December, I made plans to fly to Los Angeles for the trial. I prepared an impeccable wardrobe, wanting the jury to see me as a classy, intelligent woman.

Sometimes I awakened in the wee hours of the morning, following dreams of the glorious moment when the jury foreman would stand and pronounce the nurse "Guilty, Your Honor." My heart felt at ease with the knowledge that within a few weeks, the judge would likely impose the maximum prison sentence.

Without putting the words on paper, in my mind I reviewed the statement that I hoped to make to the court during the pre-sentencing hearings.

"That woman has ruined my life," I would tell the judge. "My finances and my health have been destroyed, and neither may recover fully due to the damage Kita Stovall has caused. If she had admitted to this travesty, I might not feel as bitter and hurt as I do today.

But the mere fact that she denied this horrendous crime signaled to me that an evil beast pulsates in her heart. Yes, it's up to God, our Creator, to impose any final judgment on her soul, but in this lifetime I want that woman to burn in hell as much as possible, at least in the sense that it's allowed by law, in prison, for as long as possible. While I realize Kita Stovall is not a financially wealthy woman by any means, she should reimburse me fully for the money she stole from me by writing the bogus checks, in addition to the credit card charges.

Your Honor, as you might very well know, this case has received extensive national publicity via reports on NBC-TV, both through the local affiliate and on the 'Today

Show'. Since then, many journalists have contacted me requesting interviews.

Many curious reporters have asked me what lessons I think people should learn from this story. I respond by telling journalists to let the public know that 'It can happen to you.' No matter who a person is, whether their income is large or small, they can become victims of predators such as Kita Stovall.

At this point, I want the court to know that I am a changed person in almost every way. Since the day I awakened from a drug-imposed stupor in a hotel room, I have developed extreme symptoms of post traumatic stress disorder, the same type of affliction that impacts veterans of military combat.

Like almost every American woman approaching her senior years, I spent the first six decades of my life in a continual quest for happiness. As everyone does, I suffered the ups and downs that life throws at us all. In my early twenties, I survived seven critical surgeries as a dedicated team of doctors worked hard to save my life, ridding my body of malignant cancers.

Despite those severe hardships, I persevered to become a successful fashion model within a highly populated regional market. Then, when terminal cancer struck my mother when I was just twenty-eight years old, I lost my house and my career when I returned to my parents' home to provide primary care for her.

Undaunted, I rebounded during my thirties and into my early forties, emerging as a major figure in the beginnings of what today has become a huge weight loss industry, so common now that many people take it for granted.

Your Honor, I know it's likely that you've seen the file I sent to the court, documenting the countless letters from my many friends and former work associates, all of them testifying to the high quality of my character and of my professionalism.

I only say this to let the court know what I was, and what I have become. Once a steady, solid person, I always somehow persevered in the face of adversity. That has all changed, at least temporarily, because of what that nurse did to me.

Besides feeling violated, I've suffered from severe hysteria, a primary symptom of post traumatic stress disorder. Many people who have known me might say that my behavior became bizarre. At times in the past few years, my speech has rattled non-stop, to the point some people become convinced that I've gone crazy.

I even started driving erratically, unable to concentrate on driving more than a few minutes at a time. Unable to eat, my weight plummeted, and several of my concerned friends volunteered to stay at my house round-the-clock.

Also, before all this began, I already suffered from extreme digestive disorder. Those symptoms worsened to critical levels as my weight rapidly decreased, I lost control of my bodily functions several times, causing embarrassing situations that no one should have to hear about, especially not in a distinguished court of law such as this.

Added to this, my personal finances suffered a tremendous loss, to the tune of nearly one and a half million dollars, mostly in medical expenses, on top of the twenty-two thousand three hundred dollars in forged checks that started this all. Your honor, if you haven't done so already, you can review documented specifics on those money totals. It is included in the informational package that I sent to the court.

Another thing that I would like to stress here is the personal advice that I would give to any woman who considers getting a face-lift or a breast enhancement. For them, it should all come down to one word, at least at the start, 'Beware.'

Do your homework beforehand. Before agreeing to such surgery or paying for it, check with the doctor's office to see what type of post-operationve care it provides. Ask who will provide nursing services, if any, and how and when those should be paid for. And have friends or family check on you immediately following the surgery as well. Yes, it's better to be safe than sorry.

And who is Kita Stovall? Who exactly is this wretched woman, now a convicted felon? What chance at leniency should she have? Frankly, I'd like to say that her background doesn't matter at all because this person deserves no mercy.

Despite my extensive research, which helped result in this conviction, I never once tried to delve into the nurse's background, because it doesn't matter one iota. What matters, to me, is what she did, her selfish actions. I could care less if she lives in a dilapidated mobile home or in a mansion. I also could care less if she behaves sweetly to people, or if she's always manipulative in her interactions with others.

All I know for sure is what happened to me, and that's a travesty. A travesty. That's what I always call it, something wretched and violating that no other human being should have to endure.

"In summary, Your Honor, I would only be satisfied to hear the maximum sentence imposed on Kita Stovall. Once again, I would like to stress that she deserves to rot in jail for as long as possible. Your Honor, I would like to thank you for your time."

After making this statement, I would hope to see this convicted felon, Kita Stovall, burst into tears, begging for mercy. Only my friends, close acquaintances and relatives would know how much this has truly changed me.

Throughout my entire life, I have always envisioned situations beforehand, largely so that I could react in a way that resulted in a successful outcome.

However, one thing that I had not expected was a phone call that I received on Monday, December 3, 2007, the scheduled first day of jury selection.

"Mrs. Shepherd, this is Mr. DeNiro, Chief District Attorney for Los Angeles," he said.

I sat on my dining room chair, my heart already fluttering because the tone of his initial statement was definitely not good.

"Yes, what happened?" I asked.

"I'm afraid the charges against Kita Stovall have been dropped today, because there's insufficient evidence."

Stunned, I dropped the receiver to the floor, and then picked it back up.

"What!" I felt betrayed. "What!"

"Mrs. Shepherd, I'm so sorry, but there was nothing we could do about it. The woman hired a good attorney, and we determined that it would have been almost impossible to convince a jury beyond a reasonable doubt as to what actually occurred."

Back in the fighting mode I instantly recapped the evidence, documents and written statements that I had compiled and supplied to the authorities. I also stressed that if the detective and the district attorney would have listened to me, and subpoenaed items that I had suggested, the criminal case would have been rock-solid.

At this point, the district attorney started making weak excuses, speaking in legalese about how those efforts would have been impossible. He said thank you in as cordial a manner as possible before our conversation ended.

A broken and shattered woman, my heart and soul torn apart, I then fell to the kitchen floor of my home, curled up into a little ball, and began wailing, yelling and weeping from the bottom of my soul. Eventually, I found myself in my bedroom, still sobbing, under the covers.

During the next few days, the phone rang on occasion as did the doorbell. I stayed in my room, unable to think straight for any lengthy period of time.

Starving and weak, on the third day after the call, I finally managed to eat a small bowl of soup and a few crackers. As my strength slowly returned, my life-long fighting spirit began to reappear.

"I'm going to fight this thing," I told myself. "I'm not going to give up, ever, and I'm going to see my finances rebound. I need to help society, and to do that I'm going to get the word out that people such as me can be strong and persevere, even in the face of our failed criminal justice system and our faulty medical industry."

That day, the third day after receiving that fateful phone call, I promised myself that I would write this book, that I would get the word out to anyone who would care to listen to or read my story.

As the days passed, I began to write my recollections, honestly reflecting on my life, so that others could discover my unique story in this book. As the weeks turned into months, I started speaking with more and more people.

Word soon spread about this book and an increasing number of journalists and everyday people began to inquire about my story. Rest assured, despite many difficulties the past several years, I remain a humble person. This will never change.

As funds from these ventures begins to flow in, I am continuing to pursue my goals including starting a non-profit charity for people with digestive disorders, and creating scholarships for veterinary students, while also expanding my doggie bed and poster businesses.

Imagine the gratitude I have felt when people and corporations began asking me to travel our country to give motivational talks, telling anyone who might care to listen how to overcome adversity and to achieve their dreams.

Yes, our country was founded by fighters and revolutionaries who stood up for their strong beliefs, for what is right and just, for the rule of law, and for the opportunity to succeed in life.

That is exactly the kind of person that I am, and that I always will be.

And rest assured, from now on whenever I awaken for the remainder of my life, I will always be alert and clear-minded, unlike on that fateful morning in the Los Angeles hotel room several years ago.

ABOUT THE AUTHOR

Margie Shepherd truly came out of nowhere. She climbed the corporate ladder in the weight loss industry and taught the meaning of appearance, self-empowerment, and above all, self-confidence to others.

Upon retiring in the late 1980s, Shepherd had established 25,000 jobs for people in five mid western states, on behalf of NutriSystem®.

A larger-than-life personality, and using her own personal methods for success, she achieved the Number One most profitable areas in gross dollars within the industry throughout the United States.

Eighteen years after retiring Shepherd decided to step back into center ring, building two companies and a charitable foundation, when suddenly she became a victim of corporate America as featured in this book.

Now a motivational speaker in global demand, she lives in Reno, Nevada.

"WINNERS NEVER QUIT, QUITTERS NEVER WIN!"

-Margie Shepherd
2010

Edwards Brothers Malloy
Oxnard, CA USA
May 1, 2013